D0122467

MRS.
RAVENBACH'S
WAY

MRS.
RAVENBACH'S
WAY

WILLIAM M. AKERS

Illustrations by Anna Wilkenfeld

Regan Arts.

Regan Arts.

65 Bleecker Street
New York, NY 10012

First Regan Arts hardcover edition, March 2016.

Library of Congress Control Number: 2015930626

ISBN 978-1-941393-58-1

"My Papi," "My Teacher," and "Cruel" © 2016 Richard Beban

Interior design by Daniel Lagin
Jacket design by Richard Ljoenes and Anna Wilkenfeld
Jacket and interior art by Anna Wilkenfeld

Printed in the United States of America
10 9 8 7 6 5 4 3 2

DEDICATION

To the finest teachers on the planet!
Esty Foster. Barbara Griffin. Lucille Maddox. Del Coggins.
Virginia Hollins. Hamilton Hazlehurst. Robin Smith. Bart Allen.
Rance Mosley. Beverly Roberts. Marc Lavine. Ann Wheeler.
Especially the *incredible* Ken Robinson.

and to

The late, amazing John Seigenthaler, the late, amazing Tom Seigenthaler, Jon Amiel, Hillary Schoelzel, Ken Kwapis, Margaret Matheson, Kristina Lyons, Harvey Burrell, and Mariel Toussaint.
Because you gave me hope.

UN-DEDICATION

Mrs. Patton, sixth grade English. After you taught me teachers betray confidences, it took me until graduate school to have a conversation with another teacher.

Mr. Burgos, upper school head. You fooled the administration, but not the students. Among other things, thanks for hauling me out of Assembly and screaming at me in front of the whole school. Most kids don't learn what morons some grown-ups are until a lot later.

Awful teachers everywhere, may you boil in oil and your eyes melt and run down your face. You know, kind of like in *Raiders of the Lost Ark*.

There. That felt good.

"It is very important that this book not be read by children. It would give them the wrong impression of their teacher. Actually, ha-ha, it would give them the correct impression of their teacher, which is not what the teacher is wishing to have happen. Do not let this book fall into the hands of the young children. It is not a good idea."

—**Mrs. Leni Ravenbach**
  Teacher, Fourth Grade
  Winner, 4 Golden Apple Awards for Excellence in Teaching
  McKegway School for Clever and Gifted Children

"What kid couldn't use a Balao-class submarine and a bunch of flamethrowers? You kidding? Who wouldn't want to blow up their teacher?"

—**Toby Wilcox**
  Student, Fourth Grade
  McKegway School for Clever and Gifted Children

"We are Chermans—we haff no superiors."

—**T. C. Boyle,** *The Big Garage*

MRS.
RAVENBACH'S
WAY

CHAPTER 1

I am a German woman. A wonderfully German woman. I teach the fourth grade. I love my students and they are loving me. My students are the most important thing to me in this world. My classroom is a place to be happy, a place to learn, a place to make the friends, a place to get to know the teacher. Nothing is quite like a classroom with everything in its place. Everything in order. Beautiful, delightful order. Nothing is more important than the order. The order, and the discipline.

My classroom is a sacred temple. It is where I do my work. In a way, it is my religion. And if any pupils get in the way of my religion, of course, sometimes I am forced to crush them.

* * *

THE CHILDREN CAME IN FROM THEIR RECESS ALL FLUSHED and joyful with anticipation for the afternoon learning. They were always learning well after the recess except for the ones who fell asleep. Soon they all had taken their places at their little shiny desks with their little shiny ears and their little shiny minds ready for the knowledge that I was about to pour into their empty little brains.

This was my favorite part of the entire fourth grade year.

I said, "Now we start the spring semester! We are beginning the writing of our journals! You shall be joining James Boswell, Ralph Waldo Emerson, Virginia Woolf, and Johann Wolfgang von Goethe, the greatest journal writers in history. Your thoughts are sacred. Anything you wish to write in your personal, confidential, private journal, it will be for you and you alone. Any thought that you have on any subject under the sun, anything at all you feel important enough to write down, you write it down."

The children were looking up at me with their eager little eyes, their fat little pencils clutched in their fat little fingers, all ready to open up their stiff new composition books and begin their journals.

Except for young Tobias Wilcox, the new boy, *natürlich*. He was staring out the window and sticking a pencil eraser into his nose. Heaven only knows what else had been up inside that very same nose! I would never want to write with a pencil that had belonged to Tobias Wilcox.

It was early in January, and young Tobias Wilcox had transferred from some awful school in some wretched city to the McKegway School for Clever and Gifted Children with all the energy of a dirty, overweight little tornado. He was not as fat as some children, of course. In fact, his parents might have not even noticed he was fat at all. His friends, if he had any friends, might also not have noticed that he was fat. But I am a fourth grade teacher, and I notice *everything*.

I am *not* fat.

I am German.

"Your journaling will lead you to the most wonderful moment in the entire school year here at the McKegway School for Clever and Gifted Children. Your journaling will take you straight to the glory of . . . the All-School Poetry Contest!"

The children cheered. Well, not all. Tobias Wilcox was pushing his pencil another inch deeper into his skull.

"Partway through the semester you will begin to write your *own* poems to recite at the year-end Poetry Contest, and the material from these poems will come from your journal! You may write about anything that pleases you. You may write about a favorite childhood memory. You may write about your favorite pet animal, your favorite stuffed animal, your favorite pet relative, your favorite stuffed relative. Ha-ha. I made a little joke."

Everyone, save Tobias, laughed because I am amusing.

"All of you must now write in your journals for thirty minutes about anything that comes into your mind, and then put them in your desk and we shall all go and see the sixth grade play. I remind you that no one will see what you write. Your journal will be yours to keep and take home with you at the end of the semester. All right, writers! It is time for you to pick up your pencils. It is time for you to write in your composition books. Thirty minutes by the clock: *eins, zwei, drei*, go!"

Other than the comforting sound of my antique ivory knitting needles going *click, click, click,* nothing is quite like the sound of a roomful of Number 2 pencils busily, happily, wonderfully scratching away on lined composition paper. All those wonderful thoughts flowing like little rivers from those tiny little brains. *Wunderbar!*

Toby Wilcox
My dumb journal
This is sooooooooooo
stooopid!

I HATE JOURNAL WRITING. I ALREADY KNOW WHAT I THINK ABOUT STUFF. DUHH. IT'S DUMB TO WASTE TIME TO WRITE IT DOWN. I COULD BE WATCHING THE CARTOON NETWORK. OR PLAYING BASEBALL. OR PICKING MY NOSE AND WIPING IT ON ARTHUR'S SHIRT.

I miss my old school. Even the teachers. Some of them, anyways. And my compadres. How can I be expected to survive? Especially Carleton. I still can't believe he's not here.

Having to leave stiiiinks. If I ever have a job and kids, I swear I'll quit before I take them outta their school and away from their buddies.
Just when Carleton and I were 2 days from finishing the most amazing tree fort in the history of the universe, I had to move to this pit of eternal boredom.

Drusie's sitting in the front of class. She looks like she'd be fun to hang out with. She smiled at me. Maybe.

I think.

I hope.

I set down my knitting and walked around. The children were biting their little thumbs, biting their little lips, furrowing their little brows. Each one thinking, and working, and writing, and sweating, and enjoying the wonderful process of putting thought onto paper for time immemorial.

I noticed in the back corner, young Tobias Wilcox was writing nothing. *Nichts.* Why was I not surprised?

I HATE JOURNAL WRITING. I ALREADY KNOW WHAT I THINK ABOUT STUFF. DUHH. IT'S DUMB TO WASTE TIME TO WRITE IT DOWN. I COULD BE WATCHING THE CARTOON NETWORK. OR PLAYING BASEBALL. OR PICKING IT NOSE AND WIPING IT ON ARTHUR'S SHIRT.

I miss my old school. Even the teachers. Some of them, anyways. And my compadres. How can I be expected to survive? Especially Carleton. I still can't believe I'm not here.

Having to leave stinks. If I ever have a job and kids, I swear I'll quit before I take them outta their school and away from their buddies.
Just when Carleton and I were a few days from finishing the most amazing tree fort in the history of the universe, I had to move to this pit of eternal

"Tobias?"

"Yes, Mrs. Ravenbach?"

"You have written nothing in your journal."

"I don't have anything to write about."

"Together you and I shall think of something *wunderbar*. When I was your age, I wrote in *my* journal about my *Grossvater*, my grandpapa. What an extraordinary man! I miss my Opa so very, very much. Reading my journal entries about my beloved Opa brings him right back to me, as if he were sitting there, sharing with me his hot cocoa and *Schnaps*. You have a grandfather, do you not?"

"I did. He died."

"Or a grandmother, perhaps?"

"Unfortunately."

"What an uncharitable thing to say!"

"She's real bossy. I don't really want to *think* about her. I sure don't want to write about her."

"No hot cocoa and *Schnaps* with *Grossmutter*? How unfortunate. Why don't you write about what excitement you have for going to see the sixth grade play, *Poppy's Grand Adventure*, this very afternoon?"

"I'm not excited."

I was unable to keep the surprise from my voice when I said, "Please? Excuse me?"

"It's a school play made by kids in school. I've never seen a good one, and I've been to a ton."

"Perhaps the plays at the school which you have attended last semester, perhaps those plays were . . . less than wonderful. At the McKegway School for Clever and Gifted Children, school plays are *always* wonderful. I'm sure when you see the play, you will change your mind."

"I doubt it."

"I've seen the rehearsals. It's quite thrilling. The waterfall effect is absolutely wonderful."

"Uh-huh."

"Perhaps you could be writing about your dog. Do you have a dog?"

"Yes."

"Yes, ma'am?"

"Yes, ma'am."

"So, write about him."

"Her. I don't want to. She scratched me this morning."

"A goldfish, perhaps? They do not scratch."

"No."

"A kitten, or a cat, or a bunny rabbit, or a rooster? Do you live on a farm? Do you have pigs?"

"No."

"No, ma'am?"

"No, ma'am."

"Pigs are wonderful creatures. Highly, highly intelligent. Smarter, in fact, I dare say, than some fourth grade students I am knowing." I studied him long and carefully. He missed the irony. Fourth grade students are not the world's greatest appreciators of irony.

I said, in my most authority-figure voice, "You. Must. Write. *Something.*" We regarded each other with mutual suspicion. I think he thought I was going to smack him. I know I thought I wanted to.

As he stared at me, he picked up his pencil and began to write. *Wunderbar!* I was not the slightest bit interested in *what* the child was writing. I was only interested *that* he was writing. Something. Anything at all.

The thirty minutes flew by! It was so quiet except for the breathing, the sniffling, the pencil scratching, and the bottom scratching. With children, there is always the bottom scratching. It was such a blissful, idyllic moment that I was loath to disturb it, even to go to the gymnasium and see the wonderful sixth grade play.

I smacked my hands together so loudly that every child sat up and went, "Ow!" Clementine Gardendale was so startled, she fell out of her chair. Sharp, sudden noises get the attention of children *so* much quicker than gently saying, "Class ... ?" When I had their complete attention, I said, "Class, it is time for the sixth grade play."

Fire in the theater! This is not a drill! Head quietly to the exits! Do not take backpacks or other belongings! Get out of this dumb excuse for a play as fast as you can and pray you don't dream about it!

THE LIONEL T. MCKEGWAY JR. SCHOOL
FOR CLEVER AND GIFTED CHILDREN

PRESENTS

MRS. DARWIN'S SIXTH GRADE STUDENTS
IN A WITTY FARCE COMEDY

Poppy's Grand Adventure

A 6th grade Play

written by Nolan Hardewick, Lauren Gidley, Bailee Risenhoover, Colby McColl, Leah Pangelinan, Kelsey Mize, and Jeffrey Amerson

directed by Mrs. Darwin herself

Act I - Was there a burglar? Night.
Act II - Where is my hat? The next morning.
Act III - A surprise for Poppy! That afternoon.

Music by Mr. Dilley's 8th grade All Trumpet Orchestra

The play was *wunderbar.*

Poppy's Grand Adventure was truly the most amazing theatrical performance I have seen in my twenty-four years of teaching fourth grade at the McKegway School for Clever and Gifted Children.

I asked the students to please raise their hand if they thought the play deserved a ten out of ten. Every student raised their hand so high, so proudly into the air, and waved it around because they all felt *Poppy's Grand Adventure* deserved a ten out of a possible ten, for a perfect score. I agreed with them heartily because the play had been so delicious and so wonderful. I was about to move on to the next part of my marvelous lesson plan when I noticed young Tobias Wilcox had not raised his chubby little hand.

I found this exceedingly strange.

I said, "Who in the class thinks *Poppy's Grand Adventure* merits a nine?" Little Tobias did not raise his hand. So I asked the class again, I said, "Who in the class thinks *Poppy's Grand Adventure* is an *eight* out of ten? Ten being the best." I was dumbfounded. Tobias did *not* raise his hand. "Who in the class, anyone in the class . . . who thinks *Poppy's Grand Adventure* is a *seven* out of ten . . . ?"

I did not understand why this little boy was *not* raising his hand. Perhaps he did not hear me. So I said to him, I said, "Tobias, do you hear me?" He nodded. Obviously he heard me; obviously he understood me. But he had not voted. I did not understand. I carefully said, "Is there anyone who thinks the play *Poppy's Grand Adventure* is a . . . *six* out of ten?"

That grinning little boy's hand shot straight up into the air! It did not make any sense. The play was obviously perfection, and sweetness, and light, and airy, and joy, and happiness, yet this peculiar little boy was giving it only a *six*. I was most amazed. The other children in the class were also most amazed.

Well, the Hackamore twins were not amazed. To be amazed by anything, they would have to be hit by a truck.

I leaned down and I said, "You are voting to give *Poppy's Grand Adventure* a *six*?" He nodded his lumpy little head. I could tell he was being intentionally rude just from the way he nodded.

He said, "Or a five." I must tell you, he had the nastiest tone of voice I have ever heard. Nasty, nasty, nasty. It was all I could do to keep from slapping him across his nasty little sticky face.

For twenty-two years now, I have taught fourth grade, and I can tell you this: That child, with his headstrong attitude and unpleasant disposition, he was headed straight for the penitentiary. I'd seen it before, trust me.

He was still looking at me. I turned away. I was preparing to give my finest lecture of the entire year, on Mr. Carter's amazing discovery of Tutankhamun's tomb. My most favorite word in the world is "wonderful," because it is what Mr. Carter said when they asked if in the tomb he could see anything. He said, "Yes, wonderful things." The fourth grade is all about seeing and learning wonderful things.

I was striding back to my desk, ready to take out my green leather-bound lecture book and do my thrilling PowerPoint presentation about Mr. Carter and the wonderful things he saw inside Tutankhamun's tomb. I was the happiest teacher in the United States of America, and perhaps the entire world, and then . . . I heard this deep, little-boy voice behind me, scraping, like dragging a coffin across a gritty stone floor.

"Mrs. Ravenbach?" Tobias Wilcox had the *most* disgusting voice. I fastened my eyes upon him, hoping that my gaze alone would silence the impertinent youth.

I was to be disappointed.

"Mrs. Ravenbach?"

"Yes?"

"Don't you want to hear why I gave it a six?"

"Not particularly, no."

"Well, I'd like to tell you."

"Must you?"

"When I was at my *other* school, my teacher *always* wanted to hear what we thought. . ."

You can imagine my opinion of *that* teacher.

I noticed all the other children leaning forward with anticipation, hoping to hear this little boy's opinion. I had no choice but to sigh and say, "So, Tobias. Why did you give *Poppy's Grand Adventure* only a six out of a possible ten?"

"I've seen lots of plays, and it was awful. The plot was dumb, the acting was crummy, there was no suspense, and mostly it was just boring. You didn't think it was boring?"

"I should say not."

"Everybody just wandered around, waiting for the next song. There was no story."

Richard Kaliski raised his hand. I said, "Richard?"

Richard, who was a brain, said, "Toby's right. There was no conflict and no character development. Nothing but exposition and more exposition, and junk happened with no rhyme or reason. It sounded like a totally crummy first draft."

I did not know what "exposition" meant, and I certainly wasn't going to ask a child in front of a roomful of other children. I said to Richard, "You gave the play a ten."

"I changed my mind. I agree with Toby. It was a six. If that."

What I did not need, more than the other many things I did not need, like dental surgery or a bleeding stomach ulcer, was a mutiny.

"Thank you, Richard. Thank you, Tobias."

"Toby."

"I am always happy to hear what you children think. It makes for such energizing class discussion. Now. Get out your exercise books. It is time we end our conversation on *Poppy's Grand Adventure* and commence our examination of pharaoh Tutankhamun and the discovery of his wonderful tomb."

I am an excellent teacher. The subject was successfully changed. Like a jagged stone thrown in a freezing cold lake, the ripples of revolt didn't last long.

But.

I had been alerted.

Young Tobias Wilcox was a terribly obstinate little boy. Little boys who believe in the free thinking, and doing things their own way, and misunderstanding the important role of the teacher in their lives, are in danger of getting off track and must be taught that there is a better way.

The correct way.

Mrs. Ravenbach's way.

CHAPTER 2

That little boy, he was going to be the death of me.

It is my considered opinion that a child who wants to go his own way will have difficulties in the life. In fact, if things don't work out precisely correctly for him, he might end up in the penitentiary. From what I could already tell about young Tobias Wilcox, if he did not "straighten up and fly right," there was an extraordinarily good chance his little life was not going to work out precisely correctly for him. At least, that has been my experience. And experience, you will come to know, is something I have quite a lot of.

In the third grade and the second grade, and in the first grade, and of course, before that in the *Kindergarten,* everything is always wonderful for the child. Everyone loves the child and the child always does well, and the teacher always tells the child and the parents how special the child is, and the parents are happy, and the child is happy, and the teacher also is very happy. This is because preschool, *Kindergarten,* first grade, second grade, and third grade, they are easy.

A child who shows up for the *Kindergarten,* first, second, and third grade, if he can go to the toilet by himself, he can excel.

Many parents foolishly believe their *Kindergarten,* first, second, and third grade students will grow up and win the Nobel Prize.

For the fourth grade student, this is no longer true.

Fourth grade is when the schooling becomes real, when the schooling becomes difficult. It is when the students learn that they can actually fail.

Sometimes the fourth grade is a wonderful experience.

Sometimes in the fourth grade there are the tears. . . .

It depends on the child. It depends on the teacher. It depends on the classroom. It depends on the flow of the studying through the semester and through the school year.

It also depends on having no bad apples. I do not like the bad apples. Not one bit.

Sadly, that semester we did have one bad apple. Just one. But still. One is one.

As you no doubt have guessed, the bad apple's name was Tobias. His classmates (I choose the term with care, because the child had no friends) called him Toby. He never stopped fidgeting, which is normal for fourth grade boys, of course. But this child *never* stopped fidgeting. Sometimes it was aggravating to me because it disturbed the other students in their work. It upset the order and the discipline.

I called Tobias, "Tobias" because Toby was such a ridiculous name. I had grave reservations about his mother and father. What parent would ever name a child Tobias when they knew full well that his chums, if he ever had any, would be all of the time calling him Toby?

In my entire life, I have never met a child named Toby who did not need to be smacked in the face.

All they want is happy happy happy.
They don't wanna hear what you really
think. Never, ever, ever. If a kid ever
said what wuz really on his mind, they'd
have to close the school. Cause the
teachers would all drop dead of a heart
attack, I swear. If kids ever told
teachers what they _really_ think, I
bet the Teacher's Union could get
a cheep price on funerals.

She's so mean. I, however, am not mean. I am a giant among men.

That's how Mr. Coggins and Mr. Robinson and Mrs. Smith made me feel. At my old school. They were nice. And great teachers. I'da walked through fire for them. Mrs. Ravenbach, not so much. Maybe I'll change my mind. Maybe. Somehow, I kinda doubt it.

Been here a week...
Already hate my teacher.

The most powerful being in the universe is the teacher. A teacher in a fourth grade classroom is more powerful than the President of the United States of America. Even more powerful, dare I say, than the Chancellor of Germany. I love the fourth grade. I have been teaching the fourth grade for twenty-six years. I love my classroom. I love my students; and my students, as I have told you, they are loving me also.

I am particularly excited this particular spring semester because this is the most important year in my teaching life. It is the year I will possibly be receiving my fifth, my fifth, I am blushing, my *fifth* Golden Apple Award for Excellence in Teaching at the McKegway School for Clever and Gifted Children.

Everyone calls it the Teacher of the Year Award, but that is not its correct name. I have four on my mantel in my gracious home, smiling at me. Mr. Ravenbach polishes them for me. I adore them. In between the four of them, I have already a little pedestal waiting for my fifth Golden Apple Award for Excellence in Teaching at the McKegway School for Clever and Gifted Children. And so, it is very important to me that all the children have a happy semester. And that none of the students is a bad apple.

The McKegway School for Clever and Gifted Children's method of the lunchroom eating is truly ingenious. At each table there are seven children and one teacher. This allows the teacher to get to know the little children extremely well through the course of each week. After Friday, the students rotate to another table. Some weeks, I must confess, the next rotation is something I look forward to, right as I sit down to my table for lunch. On Monday.

This particular Monday was not in that grim and awful category. This particular Monday, for my table were listed three little girls, including always-beautifully-behaved Drusilla Tanner. As we know, little girls always behave, especially if you give them a long, stern, strong stare which says that, if they misbehave, you will hunt them down in the girls' bathroom and cut off all their hair.

At my table, I was also to have four little boys. Arthur Hester, whose parents should divorce, and Larry Dooling, the baseball fanatic, who were quite malleable and pleasant. Richard Kaliski, the bald-headed brain. Also at my table would be the young Tobias Wilcox. Penitentiary-bound, no doubt.

I sat down at the table with my wonderful *Kartoffelsalat* and *Würstchen*. I had carefully prepared my luncheon at home and carefully packed it in a cunning little handmade wicker picnic basket. I do not eat school food. There is nothing about American cuisine that is in any way attractive to a person of refined sensibility.

I sat at the table with my back erect, waiting for the students to arrive so I could see what each one would bring from the cafeteria line to dine upon. The three little girls, of course, brought wonderful, wonderful foods—the vegetables mostly. I do so like children who enjoy their vegetables. It is a sign of excellent parenting.

Larry and Arthur brought pizza. I gave them a *look*. Both threw their pizzas in the trash and came back each with a plate of healthy green beans. What well-disciplined, lovely children!

Richard arrived with a bowl of soup and crackers and more crackers, and I noticed he had even more crackers in his pockets. Richard was a child who was deathly afraid of being caught out in the snow on the frozen tundra pursued by wolves, and it was important to him to always have food in his pockets. Richard

I looove lunch. All ya do is line up and they give ya food! How awesome is that? Someday I wanna be a chef. I'll have a restaurant that only serves white food. The White Food Diner. Spaghetti with butter and cheese. Cream of Wheat. Cheese pizza. Cheese pizza. Cheeeeese pizza!!! Only the finest for my customers!

At lunch, maybe I can find someone to swap desserts with. Lunch will be a ton of fun.

Drusie will be at my table this week. Cool. DunkAroos for Drusie?

could always be counted upon to have something in his pocket in case the teacher ever needed a snack.

I patted my soft blond hair. I smoothed my *Dirndl*. I smoothed my napkin in my lap. My napkin was German linen from Hoffmann, the finest, finest cloth woven in the entire world. I saw young Tobias Wilcox approaching with his cafeteria tray, his fat little knees rubbing together making a slithering, squeaking, awful sound. His precarious swaying made me fear I'd soon be cleaning up a slimy mess with my neatly ironed Hoffmann napkin.

Natürlich, young Tobias was bringing a most unhealthy meal. Actually, a pile of french fries with an enormous heap of ketchup spewed all over it higgledy-piggledy. Not a vegetable in sight.

As he slumped his way toward the table, I gave him my best Teutonic glare. Much to my surprise, he ignored me.

With an obnoxious scraping noise I am sure that he enjoyed, he slid his tray on the table and glared right back at me. I was taken by surprise.

I do believe I heard Drusilla give a tiny snort of snickering.

I had never had a child glare . . .

Right.

Back.

At.

Me.

He sat his fat little bottom in his chair and continued to stare at me, and he picked up a french fry and mashed it in the ketchup until it was completely covered in the ketchup. In fact, the ketchup, it got all over his fingertips. Nasty little boy. He folded the french fry in half and stuffed it in his mouth, coating both cheeks with a massive smear of the ketchup. Into my linen napkin, I nearly vomited.

"Tobias?"

"Yes, ma'am?"

"No baseball hat at the table." He removed his grimy hat and hung it on his knee. "Thank you. Now, please wipe your mouth."

"Yes, ma'am."

And that little cretin of a boy looked me directly in the eye and wiped his stained mouth *all over his sleeve,* getting the ketchup on his shirt, which his mother had no doubt spent hours ironing. Well, his mother had more likely spent *no* time ironing it because I was beginning to think that this child was raised by wild dogs.

Then, he smiled.

I wanted to smack him.

I wanted to smack him so hard that his eyeballs would fall out and roll across the floor and be stepped on by Carmella Peabody, the fattest child in the school. That would show the other children that they did not need to be sassy to Mrs. Ravenbach. But I refrained because that sort of behavior is not what a good teacher does. Especially when the principal might see.

I glared at Tobias and said, "Where are your vegetables?"

"I don't like vegetables."

"Vegetables are God's creation. Vegetables are why we live, why we eat, why we breathe. Every child loves the vegetables. Look at every child at this table. They are all eating their vegetables. Why are you not eating your vegetables?"

His voice was quite quiet but still scratchy. "Vegetables are stupid."

"Vegetables are the most perfect food invented in the world by the gods."

"Am I allowed to disagree?"

"Anyone may disagree if, in fact, they are correct in their disagreement."

"You think vegetables are the coolest thing. I think they're not."

"*Little boy . . .*" I gave my voice a dark, ominous tone. Drusilla Tanner flinched. Tobias did not.

"I'm in the fourth grade. I used to be in third grade and before that I was in second, and first grade, and before that, kindergarten. Maybe before that, I was little, but I'm not little now."

"Tell me, young Tobias, in your life have you ever eaten a vegetable?"

"Sure. Tomato sauce on pizza." I sniffed. I have perfected a perfectly marvelous *sniff.* "And ketchup. And honey."

"Honey is made by the bees. Vegetables grow in the ground. Surely in your entire life you must have at least eaten one vegetable."

"Not knowing about it, I can tell you that."

"Young man. At once, take your plate of *Fritten* back to the cafeteria line and get yourself a reasonable luncheon, something that will nourish you for the rest of the long, long hours of education before your schooling ends for the day." That little boy, he looked at me with his big, fat, wet eyes and shook his head. His filthy dirty face whipped back and forth so hard, it's a wonder his eyes didn't pop out and go flying across the room. I wondered where Carmella Peabody was. I said, "Excuse me?"

He said, "Do you wanna be excused? Bathroom's down the

hall." Bald-headed Richard laughed. Every other child at the table had the intelligence to keep very, very quiet.

I gave young Tobias my most withering stare. To my displeasure, he did not melt like the Wicked Witch of the West at the sad, sad end of that movie.

I said, "Replace your luncheon with something nourishing that will give you the strength to get you through the rest of the day. I have noticed that, on occasion, in the afternoon, the children have a tendency to droop."

"I wanna eat my french fries. That's why I got 'em. I like french fries. My mother lets me eat french fries, and you're not my mother."

"I am your *teacher*. In order of veneration, it should be: mother, father, teacher, God. No doubt your parents have taught you that. I have been assured by Mr. Hertenstein, the glorious headmaster of this glorious school, that you have wise and excellent parents."

"My parents don't let me eat everything I want at home, but I'm at not *at* home and I wanna eat french fries for lunch and I'm gonna eat french fries and nobody's gonna stop me from eating french fries because *it's a free country!*"

I could feel my blood pressure skyrocketing. The skin around my body was getting tighter. A band of wide, white pressure was squeezing around my chest and there was a brilliant stabbing pain behind my eyes.

In all my years of teaching, not since Fast Eddie LeJeune have I had a student look at me the way this young child was looking at me. A look so filled with bitter hatred toward his kind and caring teacher that I nearly fainted dead away there on the McKegway School for Clever and Gifted Children cafeteria floor. Only the thought of winning my fifth Golden Apple for Excellence in Teaching kept me upright, because as I knew full well, the fainting is a sign of the weakness, and teachers who show the weakness do not win their fifth Golden Apple for Excellence in Teaching at the McKegway School for Clever and Gifted Children.

I gripped the greasy cafeteria table with my strongest, strongest grip. I did *not* faint. I said, "You go to the serving line right this minute. Discard the french fries and *bucket* of ketchup you have put upon them and replace them with a suitable meal. Preferably of the vegetables."

I hesitate to call a child, especially a wonderful student in my own homeroom, a "snot-nosed little tub of sass," but, sadly, in this case . . . That snot-nosed little tub of sass shook his head, and said in a most displeasing scratchy little voice, "I will not."

I heard Richard whisper, "Home run, Toby." Tobias grinned at the childish encouragement and I gave Richard *the look.* Instantly, he wished he'd never spoken. Instantly, he wished he'd never even *met* young Tobias Wilcox. He bent down and began slurping up his soup, hoping I would not look at him again for the next four or five years. At least.

Tobias had openly defied me. *Me!* His teacher, *Mrs. Ravenbach.* In all my twenty-three years of teaching, I've never seen a child respond in such a way. Not even Fast Eddie LeJeune.

Because of Tobias's ghastly manner, I naturally felt terrible for myself, but I felt much, much worse for him. Such a thing can only lead a child down the road to depredation, wrack and ruin, and a life of misery, suffering and, most probably, the penitentiary.

Here was a child intent on *going his own way.* At that point, I must confess, I wiped a tear from my cheek.

A tear, not only for him, the snot-nosed, dirty-hat-wearing, penitentiary-bound little miscreant, but a tear for myself because this child, in his moment of need, had reached out to me in suffering with an absurd diet of french fries and ketchup and I was unable to make him see the light. My tear was for my inability to reach a student, a student who so richly needed reaching.

Or, who so richly needed a smack to the face.

A good German education teaches one that every now and then, every student benefits from a good smack to the face. One must be careful not to wear rings with large jewels when one gives a student a good smack to the face, because it will tear the skin and leave a scar, and then the parents write unpleasant letters of complaint to the school board.

Of course, in Germany, no one ever actually complains because they recognize the superiority of the teacher over the parent. "Mother, father, teacher, God" has a musical ring to it, does it not?

I was forced to spend the rest of that lunch period and the rest of that entire endless, dreary week at the luncheon table with little Tobias Wilcox, watching him smile and eat every single day a disgusting, greasy, dripping pile of french fries encased completely with ketchup. Red, bright ketchup made with Red Dye Number 2, which, as you know, causes the cancer in laboratory rats.

By Friday, at the end of a long, wretched, and difficult week, I dearly hoped young Tobias Wilcox would contract cancer, preferably of the galloping variety.

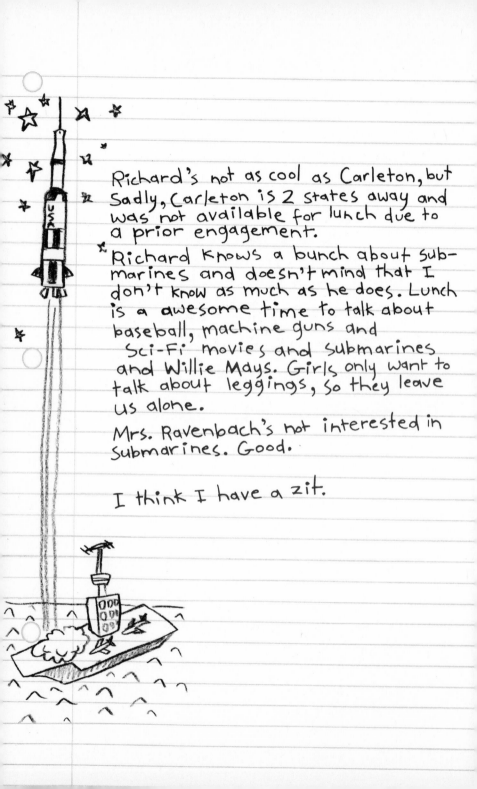

Richard's not as cool as Carleton, but sadly, Carleton is 2 states away and was not available for lunch due to a prior engagement.

Richard knows a bunch about submarines and doesn't mind that I don't know as much as he does. Lunch is a awesome time to talk about baseball, machine guns and Sci-Fi movies and submarines and Willie Mays. Girls only want to talk about leggings, so they leave us alone.

Mrs. Ravenbach's not interested in submarines. Good.

I think I have a zit.

I think Drusie really thinks Mrs. Ravenbach is a jerk. I could be badly off target about this.

Because young Tobias Wilcox's unfortunate lunchroom outburst rang a rusty bell in my distant and, I had hoped, forgotten past, it is now, with a heavy heart, that to you I must explain about Fast Eddie LeJeune.

My pupils, *natürlich*, they are all knowing *all* about Fast Eddie LeJeune. I commence every semester with a small inspirational speech about my long-ago experience with the young Edward T. LeJeune. Horror stories do get the children's attention, don't you think?

LeJeune is not pronounced "Le June" like the Army base in North Carolina. It is pronounced more like "Le Ssshun." From his last name, you can tell that Fast Eddie LeJeune was *French*. They were the enemy of my people during the Great War, and again, of course, in the Second World War. We lost both. At the World Cup time, I am not able to find myself cheering for France.

Did you know that in France, they eat the snails? Disgusting little creatures that they boil and put back into the shell. Loathsome curled-up brown bits of warm slime. Who would eat such a thing? Unimaginable. Especially when you could gobble up a nice spicy *Bratwurst*!

I was younger then and unprepared for the difficulty of instructing a child in my classroom like Fast Eddie LeJeune. It is very difficult to teach anything to anyone whose grandmother ate snails.

He, being French, or more accurately, of French descent, did not believe in the order and the discipline. Success in future life is built on the order and the discipline, and as you will see, Fast

Eddie had no success. Every day he was talking. Every day he was fidgeting. Fidget, fidget, fidget. I have never seen a child fidget more than Fast Eddie LeJeune.

Every day of that entire unpleasant year, I faced off against Fast Eddie LeJeune. It was, I have to say to you, the most difficult year of Mrs. Ravenbach's life. Well, until I met young Tobias Wilcox!

Was I right in what I felt about Fast Eddie LeJeune and the importance in a classroom of the order and the discipline? Of course I was right. Look where Edward T. LeJeune is now. Where he richly deserves to be. Rotting forever. In the *penitentiary*.

I have promised myself ever after, never to have a student in my classroom who does not believe in the order and the discipline. And progress. And good behavior. And eyes straight to the front, and hands flat on the desk, and feet flat on the floor. And absolutely no fidgeting, fidgeting, fidgeting. For you see, the fidgeting leads to the disorder, and the disorder leads to the penitentiary.

A penitentiary is a damp, dark place where they put bad children who grew into bad grown-ups. Penitentiaries are cold and grim and always made of stone. There is no television. There is no foosball. There are no video games or desserts or dolls or naps or candy bars or a mother and father to love you. There is nothing fun about a penitentiary. After one is put into a penitentiary, all one can do is to think about ways of getting out, which, of course, no one is ever able to do. The only other thing to do in the penitentiary is to wish you had been a better child and listened to your teacher so that you had not been placed in the penitentiary.

Ask me how Sick and tired and Sick and tired I am of hearing about this fast Eddie mooooooron. Who cares about Some stupe who made "inappropriate choices" and ended up stuck in prison?

Every person in a penitentiary is there because they were failed by a teacher.

Can you imagine me, Mrs. Leni Ravenbach . . . having a *second* student who went to the penitentiary? Were *that* to happen, I would never win the Golden Apple Award for Excellence in Teaching at the McKegway School for Clever and Gifted Children for the much-deserved *fifth* time.

Therefore, it will *not* happen. Tobias Wilcox will *not* be a second Fast Eddie LeJeune.

I resolved to take steps.

Fortunately, my glittery, rhinestone-encrusted cell phone was close at hand.

CHAPTER 3

The English, they are a civilized race, very good with the tea, not so wonderful when you discuss the building of the automobiles. But no matter. Tea, an English invention, or rather a Chinese invention much improved by the English; their tea is wonderful.

Like Mrs. Ravenbach! Wonderful, wonderful.

I always served tea from my beautiful Meissen teapot. My knitted-by-me tea cozy, my precious Meissen cups, earned from the first precious coins I saved from my first sunny and delightful days as a teacher. Can you imagine a fourth grade boy holding a fine porcelain teacup? Within seconds, it would be shattered on the floor! Oh, tragedy and woe!

And, I am sure, woe to that fourth grade boy.

I am good at arranging woe.

That evening, with overwhelming delight, I invited my dear friend Mrs. Button to come over for the tea. I was brimming with enthusiasm to hear the results of my phone call earlier that afternoon.

I am always so happy to welcome Mrs. Button into my home. Not simply because she thinks American football is the finest sport known to man or that her great-grandfather had the wisdom to buy Coca-Cola stock at twenty-five cents a share. And not just because she was on the board of directors of the McKegway School for Clever and Gifted Children. Of course not.

Mrs. Button is my *Freundin.*

The unkind among you would say that she is my only friend, but that is untrue. When it comes to the friendships, Mrs. Ravenbach has many. But Mrs. Button is my most especial friend. Mrs. Button understands my whims, my varying temper, my dark humors, my anger.

We look a funny pair because I'm so tall and she is so small, precisely the exact size to look a little child straight in the face and give him or her a piece of her mind. Mrs. Button and I share in common the ability to give a child a piece of one's mind. Some adults are unable to do so, but I think in those adults, that is a weakness. I dislike to repeat myself, but I am German and we have no weaknesses.

Or, very few.

My friend Mrs. Button, she is devoted to me. Sometimes I feel I am her only friend. Her husband, Mr. Button, is always working in his yard, tending his green, green grass, or taking long fishing trips. Mrs. Button has the perfect personality that you would want to have in a companion for tea.

Of course, *the most interesting* thing about Mrs. Button is that she happens to be the across-the-street neighbor of young Tobias Wilcox.

Usually I serve little cookies with the tea, but Mrs. Button had generously brought several of her delicious and prizewinning tea cakes.

At our tea, after my friend Mrs. Button and I finished discussing the most recent gifts I had been given by my pupils, I picked up my knitting and she began recounting the events that had occurred at young Tobias Wilcox's home earlier that afternoon, which I am sure will continue to be helpful to him all the rest of his days.

As my antique ivory knitting needles soothingly clickety-clicked, Mrs. Button explained how she carried a platter of exquisitely prepared, wonderful, delectable treats up their sidewalk and knocked on the Wilcox home front door.

As I poured the steaming tea into sugar in my teacup, I said, "Please. Tell all, Mrs. Button." I am not a fan of the tea bag and only a *Dummkopf* would think it superior to the loose tea.

"I have taken Mrs. Wilcox under my wing. New in town, she looks up to me and respects me. Though my children have left the McKegway School far behind, she sees me as wise and experienced in the ways of household budgeting, family, and children. I found them in the kitchen. Mrs. Wilcox, Toby, and their poorly trained dog, Godzilla. They were slouched at their messy kitchen table having after-school milk and cookies. They had to let their maid go, and it shows."

"Did they suspect your purpose in the paying of the visit?" The clickety-click was a tad more insistent.

"Fooling people is something I take pride in. Therefore, the brownies."

"I'm sure you put them 'in the know' quite quickly."

"I've always found it's good to start an important conversation

Carleton would sure as heck
know how to deal with
Mrs. Button.

by yelling, especially if you're yelling at a child. It gets their attention.

"What *did* you say? I cannot wait to hear."

"I didn't 'say.' I *screamed*. 'WHAT EVER GAVE YOU THE IDEA THAT YOUR TEACHER MRS. RAVENBACH WANTS TO HEAR WHAT *YOU* THINK ABOUT VEGETABLES?' Toby blinked. Any child who blinks is no match for an adult. His mother blinked too. She blinked a lot. 'HAVE YOU NEVER HEARD THE EXPRESSION "CHILDREN SHOULD BE SEEN AND NOT HEARD"?'

" 'Yes, ma'am.'

" 'IT'S A VERY INTELLIGENT EXPRESSION, ISN'T IT?'

" 'Yes, ma'am.'

"Then, instead of yelling, I spoke softly. But with a cutting edge to my voice, bright and razor-sharp like a Japanese samurai sword slicing through the warm entrails of a prisoner of war."

"Oh, Mrs. Button, you do have a gift for imagery."

"I said, '*Stand up* when I talk to you. Don't sit there in that chair with cookie crumbs on your shirt like a sniveling little obsequious loser. Stand up, son, and answer my *question*!'

" 'Yes, ma'am.'

"He stood right up. I grabbed his dirty little shirt and I pushed him back against the refrigerator and scooted up right in front of him until my nose was almost touching his. I had his attention. An atomic bomb could have gone off next door and he wouldn't have looked away from *me*. 'Why would you disrespect your beloved teacher?'

"He said, 'I wanted to tell her what I thought about my lunch.'

"'She's the teacher. You're the student. Why should *she* want to know *your* opinion?'

"'I don't know.'

"'Don't say, "I don't know." Answer the question.'

"'Yes, ma'am.'

"I looked at his mother. Instead of standing up and defending her child against a screeching neighbor, she just sat there holding her Oreo over her glass of milk, not dipping it, frightened like a deer when an automobile is about to mow it down. Toby's back was flat against the refrigerator and his knees were literally shaking. I thought *that* only happened in movies. It was quite satisfying to make a little boy's knees shake. Little boys' knees need to be shaken more often."

I could see that Mrs. Button was worked into, as they say, a "tizzy" telling her marvelous story about young Tobias Wilcox up against the refrigerator in his mother's kitchen while the dog barked and barked and his mother did nothing to stop her. I must say, it was an excellent and heartwarming story.

I hoped he'd been wearing short pants so she could see his knees knocking together from the fear. The fear is an excellent motivator in children. I must find a way to instill some of it in young Tobias Wilcox myself. Of course, at the McKegway School for Clever and Gifted Children they do not allow us to yell at the students nearly as often as we should.

"That awful little boy, he actually dared to speak to me. He said, 'Mrs. Button?' I said, 'Yes?' His voice was tiny and small. A voice so insignificant, it sounded like he might never speak again. He said, 'I'm really sorry.'"

"I said, 'Do you think that's going to help Mrs. Ravenbach now?! You little children think you can do *anything* you want to and just *apologize* and undo it and it doesn't *matter*! Well, let me tell you something. It *matters*! It matters *greatly*! It matters to me! It matters to Mrs. Ravenbach and the McKegway School and its board of directors that her students show proper *respect*! It matters to Mr. Ravenbach that his *wife* is not upset! It matters to Mr. Button that my *friend* Mrs. Ravenbach is not upset! I've half a mind to tell Mr. Button to take you out on his *fishing boat* to the middle of Echo Canyon *Lake* and wrap an anchor *chain* around you and drop you off in the deep, deep, cold, cold, cold *water*!'"

Mrs. Button was so worked up that she had to catch her breath and have a sip of tea. Her chest was quivering and her face was dotted with the lightest layer of perspiration. It was quite attractive, actually. For someone so small and delicate and bird-like, her shrill voice was as piercing as a fifteen-inch cannon shell from the *Tirpitz* exploding a day care center.

"Well, Mrs. Button," I said, "you certainly are articulate when you are in a rage. More tea?"

I poured.

"And what did he say?"

Mrs. Button said, "He sort of whimpered, 'Save me, Willie Mays...' And what a surprise! Willie Mays did *not* save him. Silly child. He'd have had a far better chance had he prayed to Joe Namath. Then he said, 'No, thank you,' and I said, 'No, thank you, *what*?'

"'No, thank you, I don't want... Mr. Button... to take me out on his fishing boat into the middle of Echo Canyon Lake and...

wrap an anchor chain around me . . . and drop me off in . . . the deep . . . deep . . . cold, cold water.'

"'I've come over here on my own time to try and help you grow up to be a better person, and all you can muster up to say is "No, thank you"?'

"'Thank . . . you.' He was so confused. Bonus points for me.

"'Thank you for *what*?' I asked. I could tell I was getting to him. His little knees were shivering.

"'Thank you . . . for trying . . . to help me . . .'"

I leaned forward toward my friend Mrs. Button. My big, hard, round belly was nearly touching the little table between us. My big, round bosoms nearly knocked over my precious Meissen tea pot. What a disaster that would have been! I lowered my voice and asked her, "And what did his *mother* say?"

Mrs. Button smiled like a cat that's just eaten its tenth canary. "Toby was looking at his mother. He had this scared, drowning-in-quicksand look in his eye, this imploring look of, 'Please, mother. Please help me. Please stop this unpleasant woman from speaking to me in such an unpleasant way.'"

"And, Mrs. Button, what did Mrs. Wilcox do?"

"*Not a thing.* She didn't stand up. She didn't step my way. She didn't pick up a butcher knife and shove it between my ribs. She did none of those things you might think a mother would do when her child is threatened. She just sat there with her Oreo dangling over her glass of milk like an imbecile, and allowed me to have my say. His poorly behaved dog tried to bite my ankle. I kicked it squarely in the face and it found something else to do.

"Bit by bit, I saw Toby caving in and becoming quieter. It was almost as if he was a house of cards collapsing in slow motion as he folded into himself and pulled the light in after. When I finished talking, the light inside him had without a doubt gone out, which was my goal."

"What a triumphant, uplifting story that is."

"But that's not all . . ."

"Could the story possibly improve? Oh, please, Mrs. Button, I'm aflutter with excitement."

"Well. It was a marvelous addition to my Lifetime List of Grand Achievements. I glanced down at the kitchen floor, which needed a good scrubbing, and, between his filthy dirty sneakers, I saw . . . a puddle of bright yellow pee-pee."

"Oh, Mrs. Button, you are to be congratulated! That sort of beneficial lesson will stay with him for years and years and years. I wish *I* were able to make children pee in their trousers, because then you know you have truly reached them."

I would not be surprised if, after his talk with Mrs. Button, young Tobias Wilcox never offered his opinion about anything, ever again. Ever.

Mrs. Button has that effect on children.

As she left, she said, "Do give Mr. Ravenbach my best." I promised I would.

I miss Carleton and his platoon of model soldiers. What if they was <u>real</u>? The stuff we could do with them!

THE WORLD WANTS TO BLOW UP MRS. BUTTON!

I know, I know... none of that stuff's ever gonna happen. I'm a kid. Zero power, in tighty whiteys. For one thing: who'd help me find nuns with AK-47s? Plus, machine gunning people into goo is not nice and is against the law.

What's not against the law is yelling at a kid. Anybody can do that anytime they want and nobody cares. Or stops 'em. If anybody sees a grown-up screaming at a kid, they figure the kid did whatever to deserve it. Heck, they might even help out, in case the kid doesn't quite get the point.

Jerkfaces.

It would have been better if Willie Mays had busted in with a baseball bat or Mom had said something to Mrs. Button.

In my drawing, I'm yelling. In real life, that's not what I did.

Crying stinks.

What'd I ever do to Mrs. Button? Something that pissed off her friend Mrs. Ravenbach. What? Breathing? Talking out loud?

Or does she just hate kids?

Whatever it was, I don't want to ever do it again.

What I'm going to do is I'm going to keep my big...fat... mouth... shut. Zactly like my #@$%* teacher wants.
Sigh.

Drusie was sitting at her desk and
turned around and gave me the meanest
look I've ever seen. Couldn't believe
it. She sneered at me.

Drusie sneered at me.

Sigh.

Sigh.

Google How can I get to the farthest corner of the world and never, ever come back? 🔍

Zanzibar 🔍

Anartika 🔍

Anartica 🔍

Antarktika 🔍

Antarctica 🔍

Timbucktwo 🔍

Timbucktoo 🔍

Timbuktu 🔍

plane ticket to Timbuktu 🔍

get rich quick 🔍

I'm never gonna feel good again.
Ever. And I can't tell my parents.
I can't tell anybody. Nobody cares
at all.

This stinks so bad.

Carleton's not here. And he's not
gonna be here. Ever.

Gotta do something. Gotta make
a move.

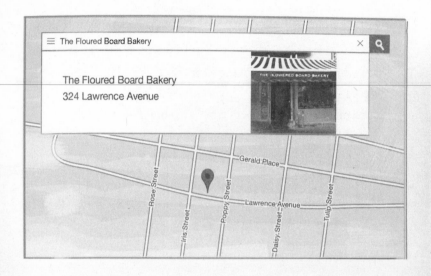

I hope this works. Mom said it was too expensive, and that you pay all that money for ambience (whatever that is) but the bread doesn't taste any better. I said it <u>had</u> to be this one. Drusie and Arthur told me it's Her favorite bakery.

If this doesn't work, I'm the one that's baked.

More like deep fried.

Outside the school was the heavy early morning rain. Inside there was the happiness, the warmth, and the sunshine. Because it was my classroom. Where I teach.

I was just reaching up to scratch the mole on my chin. It was itching. It was quite an attractive mole with lovely stiff hair growing out of it. I was quite proud of my mole. Anyone can have a perfect face. A face that can survive something as unusual as a mole with thick, bristly hair growing from it makes that person into an individual, strong character.

I was just about to scratch my mole, deeply, forcefully, which would have been quite satisfying, when I saw at the door of my sacred classroom, young Tobias Wilcox.

Early.

Extraordinarily early!

I wondered why perhaps he might have come to see me this early in the morning because normally, he was a straggler.

He was soaking wet. Imagine the kind of a parent who would let a child leave the house without a rain jacket, or a poncho, or an umbrella, or a rain suit, or something! At least a plastic garbage bag to cover himself to walk from the automobile to the school building in the drenching rain!

A puddle of water spread all across the hall floor. I prayed he would not step into my homeroom.

He stepped into my homeroom.

My blood pressure shot through the roof thinking about water stains on my precious Bokhara rug. I had purchased it at ruinous expense on a hedonistic touristic expedition to Pakistan. My Bokhara rug was one of my prized possessions and now his foul little feet were making little wet footprints as he crossed to my desk.

I did, however, notice he was carrying a crinkly paper bag with an attractive light blue logotype from the Floured Board. Mrs. Ravenbach's favorite bakery! It could not have contained his schoolbooks because it was roundish in shape.

His wet little puppy dog eyes under his wet little puppy dog hair looked up at me with the kindest, sweetest expression. My heart exploded with warmth for my adorable young pupil.

"Mrs. Ravenbach?"

"Yes, Tobias?"

"I've got something for you I think you might enjoy."

"I always like to have things that I might enjoy. What is in the bag?" What I wanted to do was grab the bag, throw it on my desk, rip it open, and find out what was inside. But that would have been impolite and a bad model of behavior for an impressionable child. More than anything, I am an excellent teacher!

"It's bread. From the Floured Board. I think it's your favorite. At least I hope it is. It's called farm bread and there's butter and strawberry jam in there too."

Since January, when I had begun teaching young Tobias Wilcox, he had never seemed quite so adorable. The expression on his adorable face was so kind and gentle and loving, it was all I could do to stop from hugging him close to my bosom and telling him what a wonderful child he was. Perhaps this was because he was giving me a gift.

I smiled only a tiny, tiny, tiny bit, and said, "Thank you, Tobias. Though it is a quite small loaf of farm bread, I certainly will enjoy eating it with Mr. Ravenbach later on this evening. He is particularly fond of the strawberry jam."

"I hope you both enjoy it."

"If you don't mind, I probably will dispense with writing you a thank-you note because I have now thanked you in person."

"Oh that's okay. I don't need a thank-you note. I'm hoping you like the bread and the jam. I bet it's really good."

He was looking up at me. His big, wet eyes, looking up at me, up, up, up. Like a puppy. Like a hungry puppy. Like a hungry puppy who hoped he would get a slice of fresh buttered bread with a thick pile of strawberry jam on it.

I thought not.

A gift is a gift, and not meant to be shared with the gift giver. That would be idiotic.

That little boy was filled with the strange looks. Lately, he was giving them to me quite often. This one was one of the strangest yet.

* * *

A WONDERFUL THING FOR THE GROWING CHILDREN IS THE exercising. It concentrates the mind. It invigorates the body and the spirit. As a student in East Germany, I always benefitted from the vigorous exercise. Now, of course, I no longer exercise. I supervise.

That afternoon, my students were at the recess. I supervised from my sunny and bright classroom while they were out in the rain doing their running. Running, running, running. Always running. In large rectangles around the playground. The other teachers' classes at the recess, they played the basketball and the soccer, but not Mrs. Ravenbach's superior students. For them, always the running. Unlike the running, the basketball does not increase the stamina or build the character. In later life, basketball is of no use. I do understand they play quite a lot of basketball in penitentiaries.

I noticed with satisfaction that the other students were in clumps, having delightful conversations, but Tobias, he was running by himself. He was slump-shouldered and looked lonely and pathetic, which I am certain he was. It may have been because of his patheticness that no one wanted to run beside him.

But, perhaps it may have been because of something else . . .

I have never yet met a child who enjoys another child who shares his or her own opinion loudly, sharply, incorrectly in the classroom, on the playground, at the lunch table, or anywhere. The *worst* thing is a child who feels that his or her own personal opinion is important, more important even than that of the teacher.

I noticed young Tobias Wilcox struggling to accelerate enough to catch up with bald-headed Richard Kaliski. After nearly a lap around the playground, and a lot of the huffing and the puffing, Tobias caught up.

Richard was the sort of a child who wore short pants in the wintertime, horizontal striped shirts long after they had gone out of fashion, and kept his hair cut completely off but was not any sort of an anarchist.

He was one of those "technokids," the children who in the class-rooms connect the computers to the projectors, and does things with the sound for the school plays, and plugs in the sixteen-millimeter projector to the speakers so that we can see the old black-and-white movies. He was a useful child to have around but did not have much to say to anyone, as far as I could tell. Richard was highly intelligent and why he chose to run with young Tobias Wilcox, the dimmest child in the history of dim children in my fourth grade classes, I shall never know.

Yet, there he was, on the playground, running and talking with Tobias Wilcox, the child who had no friends.

It was the strangest thing.

THE AUTHENTIC AND VENERABLE CAMARADERIE OF SUBMARINE ENTHUSIASTS

<u>A full report on the first official, initial inaugural kickoff meeting of the McKegway School Submarine Club.</u>

Me: Slow down, dude.

Richard: Hey.

Me: Before I ralph.

Richard: Sure.

Me: How's it going?

Richard: Better for me than you. As you are no doubt well aware.

Me: Yeah, I've never exactly been teacher's pet.

Richard: You're sure not now. I've yet to see anything like it.

Me: I feel like Willie Mays when the Giants traded him to the Mets . . . We should form a club.

Richard: No way. You'll be dead soon. She's going to kill you.

Me: There is that possibility.

Richard: I don't look good in black. Why should I form a club with you?

Me: We could build submarines.

Richard: Awesome! Stellar idea! The Sub Club! I can keep the minutes.

Me: First we design.

Richard: Then we build.

Me: Hey, while we're working, we can listen to Zip Tuggle announce the Admirals' games.

Richard: Cool . . . We could test prototypes in Lake Ruppenthal at the park!

Me: World War II subs!

Richard: Balao class!

Me: We can do illustrated articles about our progress for the McKegway Herald!

Richard: We need a logo.

Me: That, I can handle. What about a motto?

Richard: How about "Be Prepared?"

Me: Naah. Boy Scouts got that one.

Richard: "Who Dares, Wins?"

Me: But that's Special Air Services.

Richard: Who ever's heard of them? Besides us?

Me: True that.

Richard: Can you come over after school?

Me: Sure thing. Your Moms got snacks?

Richard: She's so desperate for people to like me, she's got Oreos and Warheads.

Me: Gotta like a mom that covers all the bases.

Richard: To the Sub Club!

Me: The Sub Club rules!

A fist bump sealed the deal and the Sub Club was officially in action.

On/off
Switch

Stern ballast
loading hatch

Hing-

Arth

Playmob

pirates—

Stern
diving plane

Stern diving plane

lantern
battery
6 volt

Propellor

electric
motor

Alka
Seltzer
ballast tank
plugs

Wilcox

General
Dynamics
Electric
Boat

Kaliski

Hester

Richard

Me

Windshield

Conning tower

Lead shot ballast

Bow dive plane

Forward ballast hatch

Dr Pepper buoyancy chambers

Alka Seltzer ballast tank plugs

Saran wrap

Bottle rocket torpedoes

Lead keel (from Playmobil pirate ship)

CHAPTER 4

It was half past eleven on a Monday morning as I was striding down the hallway toward my homeroom. I was enjoying the sound my Christian Louboutin high heels made on the polished concrete and the pleasant echoes as the sound ricocheted down the halls announcing my presence. The sound of heels (shoe or boot!) is always pleasant. My high heels are quite elegant and are the only thing French I am able to tolerate.

I had assigned the little children a few tasks to occupy themselves while I was away making myself a cup of good strong German tea in the teachers' lounge.

With the satisfying sound of my heels in my ears, I entered my lovely classroom. The sun outside may have been nonexistent, but inside it was all sunny and bright and beautiful.

All the children had their heads bent over their desks, writing furiously in their journals or doing their homework or reading a wonderful book. Every child, save one. And I'm certain you are able to guess which one *that* one was.

In the back of the classroom, by himself, next to my

hand-rubbed walnut bookcase, young Tobias Wilcox was perusing my collection of old yearbooks.

"Tobias!"

"Yes, ma'am?"

Young Tobias Wilcox tossed the yearbook down and scuttled like a crab across the floor, endeavoring to return to his seat as quickly as possible. I am certain that the young lad also wished he had been quite invisible. Fourth grade boys often wish they could be invisible.

Tobias's fat little bottom slapped the hard wood of his chair. I could tell he was sweating. Sweat is not a pleasant thing in a fourth grade boy.

"Why were you away from your desk?"

He said what all fat little fourth grade boys say, but in this case, with a tiny voice that sounded like it was coming from the dark side of the moon: "I didn't know I was supposed to be at my desk, Mrs. Ravenbach." But, I thought I detected a faint note of sarcasm... I drew in my breath in surprise. The *tone* of that child's voice! So snooty. So holier-than-thou. So grating. So unpleasant. So disrespectful to his adoring teacher.

It was astounding, but, evidently, true: Mrs. Button's heartfelt refrigerator lecture *had not worked*! That sweaty tub of sass, evidently, *still* ... wanted ... to go ... his own ... way.

I would see about that.

I turned my magnificent blond head to Drusilla. My *favorite* student. "Drusilla?"

"Yes, Mrs. Ravenbach? How may I help you?"

"You may help me by telling young Tobias Wilcox what the instructions were that I left for the entire classroom when I went up to the teachers' lounge to make my good strong German tea."

Drusilla stood up brightly beside her desk. "Mrs. Ravenbach, you told everybody we were to remain at our desks working quietly until you returned."

Drusilla curtsied, sat down, and folded her well-manicured hands on her desk. Her mother makes me homemade pastries and sweets and little tarts with my name in pink icing across each one. They are so beautiful, I almost hesitate to eat them. Almost. Drusilla is a sensible child, and has been gifted with a sensible mother.

"Tobias?"

"Yes, ma'am?"

"Why were you nosing about in my collection of yearbooks?"

"I was conducting a personal research project. I wanted to see what kinda clothes people wore a long time ago. They were really ugly."

I picked up the yearbook. 1993. I sniffed. I remember beginning to put together a question in my mind about why he had picked the yearbook for 1993 to root through, but the bell rang for dismissal. I replaced the yearbook on the shelf in its proper spot with all the other yearbooks and turned my magnificent brain toward thoughts of parent-teacher conferences.

Feels good to have a plan. Who Dares, Wins!

The parent-teacher conference which is beginning with the smell of the freshly baked bread is sure to be a wonderfully successful parent-teacher conference. Nothing pleases me more at the beginning of a parent-teacher conference like the crinkle of a paper bag marked "The Floured Board." Oh my, my, my, my. Because the warm, friendly, bakery-smelling, crinkly white bag marked "The Floured Board" that Tobias was holding in his nervous, chubby little hands was exceptionally large, I knew that this parent-teacher conference with young Tobias Wilcox and his mother and father was going to go exceptionally well.

I have never met a mother or a father who did not seek and value my advice on how they could better do their important job as a parent. The fact that I have no actual children of my own has nothing to do with my knowledge of pediatric behavior. All the parents know and respect this.

Because he started at the McKegway School for Clever and Gifted Children only this semester, this was the first time I had met the parents of young Tobias Wilcox. Because of the immense size of the crinkly paper bag marked "The Floured Board," it was clear they understood that a successful education is an important thing in a child's life.

Mr. Wilcox, I am sorry to report, was fat. He had a round face and a round little tummy. It would be cute on a young boy of nine or ten years old, but on a grown man it showed a lack of the order and the discipline.

Mrs. Wilcox was quite pretty, if you like that sort of look.

I had before me, on my hand-inlaid Biedermeier desk, a list of items for discussion about Tobias Wilcox, beautifully written in magenta fountain pen ink. Every single item on my desk is in perfect alignment with every other item on my desk at precisely an angle of 90 degrees to the bottom edge of the desk. So comforting to be precise. The order and the discipline, *ja!*

As you may not be aware, my desk is on a two-foot-tall platform that raises it high above the little students. It gives them a sense of well-being to know that their teacher is above them, looking down on them, watching them carefully, like an eagle inspecting its prey.

I could tell the parents were a bit nervous. It is important to be a little uneasy in front of an authority figure, especially one tall and imposing and with beautiful blond hair such as myself.

Sitting there, below me, in front of my desk, young Tobias Wilcox stared at me and stared at me and stared at me. Fortunately the eyes are not laser beams or I would have been sliced into sixteen pieces of wonderful German woman.

What I needed was a stiff riding crop I could smack on the desk each time I made an important point, which was often, knowing that the *smack* on the shining wood would certainly get the parents' attention, not to mention the attention of young Tobias Wilcox, who needed some attention-getting, I can assure you.

Sadly, I had no such riding crop. While they cowered before me, I thought about purchasing several.

I smiled kindly. "Tobias. Hat." He carefully placed his filthy headgear on his knee. "Now, Mr. and Mrs. Wilcox. I have been delighted to have your son Tobias in my classroom."

Mr. Wilcox said, "We like to call him Toby."

"I prefer Tobias. Formality is critical in the well-balanced student-teacher relationship."

"We're not very formal people," said his mother.

"Tobias, Toby never you mind. It is still the same sweet, ador-able, intelligent child. And thank you for the bread. It smells absolutely delightful and delicious."

"You're welcome," said his mother. Her name was not important.

"We are working very hard in the classroom to make your child a better student and a better citizen."

"Thank you, Mrs. Ravenbach," said Mr. Wilcox.

"We appreciate all you're doing for him," said Mrs. Wilcox.

Mr. Wilcox said, "Right, Toby?"

The child did not wish to speak and I helped him achieve *that* goal. "Mr. Wilcox, as this is a parent-teacher conference and not a parent-teacher-pupil conference, I do believe we can dispense with remarks from young Tobias." Tobias shrank back in his chair. Good little fellow!

"It is fascinating and wonderful and quite to the point that you are bringing the bread to this parent-teacher conference when I must be discussing with you the nutrition, and young Tobias's eating habits."

"Toby eats just fine," said Mr. Wilcox.

"He's right in the middle for all his height and weight percen-tiles," Mrs. Wilcox smiled. She was quite proud of her son's being average. How sad.

American parents will allow their children to eat anything, willy-nilly, just to leave the parents in peace. Most parents in America would give their children a nose bag of sugar if they thought it would keep them quiet for five minutes. I said, "Are you aware that young Tobias at lunchtime only eats the french fries with the ketchup—and may I say, quite an enormous amount of ketchup?"

"It's hard to make him eat," said Mrs. Wilcox.

I thought to myself, It's hard to make him eat delicious, nutritious food! Getting roly-tummy Tobias Wilcox to eat the junk food, a one-legged retard could do that! To Mr. and Mrs. Wilcox, I did not say these things out loud. I did say, "I have asked him, on several occasions, to replace his french fries with something more nourishing. Such as the vegetables." The disgusted expression on Tobias Wilcox's face nearly made me laugh, but it is bad form to laugh at a student unless he or she is throwing up. "What is reflected in his eating habits, Mr. and Mrs. Wilcox, is that your child is exhibiting disturbing signs of the disobedience and the headstrongness and the freethinking. At the McKegway School for Clever and Gifted Children, this is behavior we are not encouraging. The students must understand that it is their teacher who is knowing the best way for them to be doing their thinking. If we do not follow our good role models, how *can* we learn, I ask you?"

"Well . . ." said Mrs. Wilcox.

"Well . . ." said Mr. Wilcox.

I decided it was time to be honest with them.

"Mrs. Wilcox, Mr. Wilcox, young Tobias." My voice was the teeniest bit . . . *harsh.*

"Please call him Toby. That's what he likes," said Mr. Wilcox.

I could see Mr. Wilcox sweating the teeniest bit above his eyebrows. In a parent-teacher conference, I like a parent who sweats. It means they are paying attention.

"Of course I shall be happy to call him Toby. Whatever

pleases him. Now, it is very important that you listen very, very carefully to what I am about to say because it truly, truly matters."

Mr. Wilcox leaned forward. Mrs. Wilcox leaned forward. Young Tobias Wilcox leaned back. I lowered my voice until it sounded as if it had been dipped in the acid and was being dragged across a slaughterhouse floor.

"If Tobias . . . does not straighten up and, as they say, 'fly right,' he will *not be allowed to progress to the fifth grade.*"

There followed a longish pause. Quite a longish pause, actually.

They sat there blinking. Like the dumb animals before the slaughter.

"Huh?" said young Tobias Wilcox. Even his "huh" sounded dull-witted.

"Excuse me?" said Mr. Wilcox.

"We didn't realize he was doing that poorly," said Mrs. Wilcox.

The parents, they never do.

"Mr. and Mrs. Wilcox. I spoke clearly, if admittedly with a slight, if elegant, German accent, but I'm sure you understood me. However, I am happy to repeat myself. If your child continues to behave in this incredibly headstrong and, may I say, belligerent manner, young Tobias will fail in his education and will be compelled to repeat the fourth grade."

Oh no.

It was as if, in the classroom, I had set off a satchel charge. After the explosion, so quiet and peaceful.

It is so satisfying to get a parent's attention and, I must say, it is even more satisfying to get the attention of a fat little fourth grade boy.

I sure had Toby's.

CHAPTER 5

It was the most beautiful kind of a day. The sun came streaming through the squeaky-clean schoolroom windows, shining a gorgeous warm light on every child, heads bent down industriously writing in their personal journals. As I knitted, the sound of the fat pencils scratching on the paper filled the room, as you could almost *see* the thought and the care and the precision with which each child was writing in his or her own private diary.

It warmed my heart to watch every child, head bent submissively, dutifully, carefully writing their innermost thoughts, spilling them on the page for no one at all to read.

Even Tobias.

I don't think in all my days as a teacher I'd seen a child write with such passion. It warmed my heart, as I said, to watch young Tobias work, knowing that it was I who had inspired him to write his thoughts in his journal so well and so lovingly.

It is a wonderful thing to be that one teacher who makes a child step across the little stream from one side to the other, from childhood to grown-upness, knowing that many years from now,

This is soooooo incredibly stoooopid.
Blah blah blah blah blah blah blah
blah blah. I hate poems. And poets.
Blah blah blah blah blah blah blah
blah blah blah blah blah! And teachers
and school. Blah blah blah blah blah
blah blah blah blah blah blah blah
blah blah blah blah blah blah blah
blah blah blah blah blah blah blah blah
blah blah blah. And teachers who make
you write poetry. Yukko city. Blaaahh.
Yikes. Brakes! Skidding!
ERRRRRRRRRR. CRASH.

the child will look back and think to himself or herself, "Mrs. Ravenbach turned me around. She made me what I am today. Mrs. Ravenbach is a hundred percent responsible for all of my successes. Had I not had Mrs. Ravenbach in fourth grade at the McKegway School for Clever and Gifted Children, I too, like Fast Eddie LeJeune, might have ended my days behind the cold stone walls of a penitentiary!"

Wunderbar!

From time to time, young Tobias Wilcox would silently mouth some words, stare at the wall, thinking deep, profound, impressive thoughts. I must say it gave me a *Schauer* (which means a shiver, a delightful shiver) to think it was I who had led this child to do such wonderful work. I knew the work he was doing was wonderful because he was writing with such speed. Children who write rapidly in their journals are connecting their hearts to the page. You cannot imagine the warmth of the feeling that swelled up inside me as I watched young Tobias Wilcox write and write and write and write and write.

Oh, what a wonderful poem it was going to be!

The All-School Poetry Contest at the McKegway School for Clever and Gifted Children is, as I am sure you are well aware, one of the greatest events in the school year. It trumps the Easter Egg Hunt, the Barbecue Flop, the Glorious Christmas Concert, the Halloween Pageant, even, to be completely truthful, German Pastry *und Strudel* Day.

The All-School Poetry Contest is a time for the luckiest teachers to shine, because their students will stand before the entire school and recite a splendid poem of their own devising. Such a sweet moment for the student, such a proud moment for the teacher.

As you know, each child must recite their poem in front of his or her grade. The winner of each grade goes on to recite the poem in front of all of the students, the principal, the alumni, the parents, adoring grandparents, teachers, and even the custodial staff, such is the magnitude and importance of the McKegway School for Clever and Gifted Children All-School Poetry Contest!

None of my students had ever won the Poetry Contest.

It was a black, sticky spot on my Permanent Record. Were one of my students to be crowned the King or Queen of Poetry, I would most *certainly* be awarded a much-deserved fifth Golden Apple Award for Excellence in Teaching!

At the day's end, the little children closed their grubby little journals with their grubby, fat little hands, smearing them with jelly and dirt and God knows what all as they replaced them in their desks.

They gathered their book bags, their textbooks and notebooks, their pens and their pencils, and their clear plastic rulers, and trooped slowly from the classroom out to the carpool line and their parents' car, sporting events, karate classes, piano lessons, other mindless after-school activities, home, homework, dinner, more homework, more homework, and then at last: bedtime, blissful bedtime . . . sleeping peacefully, dreaming gently, serene in the knowledge they had told their private journals everything there was to possibly tell.

Trevania Sumner traipsed out the door, her little skirt twitching just enough for me to see her frilly white underpants. She went into the hall and I was alone in the classroom for the first time since the morning.

An empty classroom is a joyous and wonderful thing.

The first thing I did was to put on my lipstick. I have Ovid Schiesser Nr. 03 imported from Germany, as I am sure comes as no surprise to you. I straightened my hair. I straightened the lace around my cuffs. I straightened the lace around my collar. I stood up. My elegant Christian Louboutin high heels made a *tac, tac, tac* as I regally walked toward the desk of young Tobias Wilcox.

When I opened his desk, *Gott im Himmel*, what a revolting mess. I shoved through piles of untidy paper until I found, first, a half-eaten peanut butter and jelly sandwich, second, a dead centipede, and third, his personal journal.

I carefully removed his journal and carefully carried it back to my desk, where I laid it out lovingly on the warm, shining wooden surface of my beautifully varnished Biedermeier teacher's desk.

I reflected for a moment.

It was time to amplify my effort to help young Tobias Wilcox to stay out of the penitentiary.

As I reached my well-manicured and soft hand gently toward the cover of Tobias Wilcox's personal journal, my heart fluttered. I was filled with a feeling of love and affection for that little boy unlike any I had felt before. I was going to peer into his innermost thoughts. I was going to reach my hand in, like God reaching to his soul, to praise him and help him to become the person he needed to be, launched forward from the fourth grade classroom of Mrs. Leni Ravenbach into the wonderful fullness of life.

I felt at peace.

I cracked my knuckles. It sounded like a bamboo forest breaking in two.

I opened his journal.

I began to read.

Because German is my native language, when I am reading the English, my lips move a tiny bit. It is for this reason I read only when I am alone. I don't want the little children to poke fun.

The more I read the journal of young Tobias Wilcox, the faster I moved my lips because the more I read, the faster I went. I read so quickly, it was as if my lips were on fire. The wonderful things I hoped to discover, the delightful thoughts I had been expecting with all my heart, they were not there.

She's the meanest teacher in the history of the universe. Mrs. Ravenbach can't even teach. Nothing she says makes sense. And she doesn't care. She thinks it's funny that nobody understands her lessons. If she's so awful, why do they let her work here? Has she got video of someone doing something they shouldn't have and is threatening to put it on YouTube? Huh?

She's the Queen of Awful. She Who Must Be Obeyed. The Lucifer of Teachers.

"Off with her head! Do you hear me! Off, off, off!"

I'd like to put her in stocks, like when they had the Salem witch trials and stuff, in front of the whole town, and have the village elders hack her hair off with dull scissors and then shave her head with a rusty razor and then while the band played a Beatles song, all the ancient wrinkly old men would line up and pull down their pants and fart in her face!

Kids'd come from miles around and pay a month's allowance to watch that! Awesome!

How could this be? How could this *possibly be*?

Tobias Wilcox *was* working on his poem for the All-School Poetry Contest, the little beast.

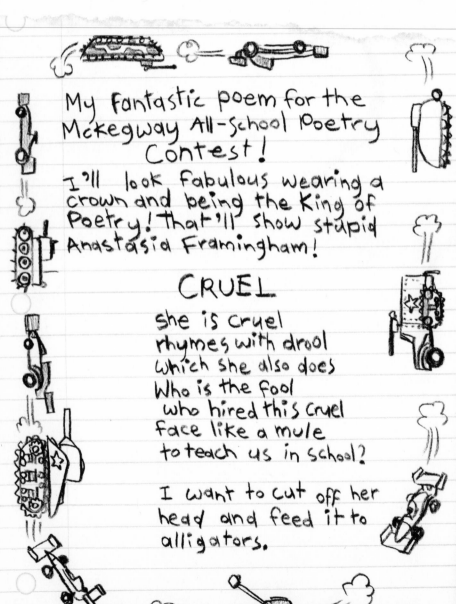

My Fantastic poem for the Mckegway All-School Poetry Contest!

I'll look fabulous wearing a crown and being the King of Poetry! That'll show stupid Anastasia Framingham!

CRUEL

she is cruel
rhymes with drool
which she also does
Who is the fool
who hired this cruel
face like a mule
to teach us in school?

I want to cut off her head and feed it to alligators.

I read his entire journal.

No wonder he had been writing so fast. Every single ghastly page was *all* about the terrible things he wanted to do to me! Mrs. Leni Ravenbach, his *teacher*! It was a truly a terrible, awful, nasty, disgusting, loathsome little journal!

Never before in the twenty-seven years of my teaching had I actually hated a child, but I *hated* little Tobias Wilcox!

What was particularly upsetting about the entire unfortunate event was the way Tobias Wilcox had managed to shatter my perfect mood, my exquisite moment of joy and happiness. When I opened his composition book and started to read his journal, I was filled with love and care and affection for the fat little freak. That warm feeling had been shattered like a gigantic Steuben cut-glass vase falling to a marble floor and smashing into a thousand trillion sharpened pieces ready to jab into the bare foot of any unsuspecting passerby. From happiness to shattered glass!

Because of that horrible, horrible, horrible child!!

I quickly crossed my sunny, light-filled homeroom, opened Tobias's desk, and thrust his journal inside. His desk looked like an infected sewer. I was certain that if I peered closely I would find a dead rodent or perhaps a severed hand.

It is critical for the good teaching that the student never suspects the teacher is reading his or her private journal. That defeats the purpose of the journal! Every teacher knows that, when you have finished reading a student's personal, confidential, private journal, it is crucial to place the journal inside the student's desk in *exactly* the exact same place from where one removed it. Young Wilcox's desk was such a foul, repulsive mess, I could have hidden a live rhinoceros in there and he never would have noticed.

What I should have *liked* to have hidden in his desk, of course, was a hungry boa constrictor, but I felt it would not be in good taste and might be harmful to the boa constrictor.

CHAPTER 6

Tragically for me, during the long, long evening that followed, I was not able to make my sad mood go away. Even drinking with Mr. Ravenbach three bottles of the finest Spätlese Riesling wine had not helped. Well, it helped some.

To make the matters worse, when I arrived at my classroom the next morning, not only was I still sad, but I had a headache the size of Neuschwanstein Castle. Unfortunately, my headache was not as pretty as Neuschwanstein Castle.

Soon, the children flooded in, flushed, excited, red-faced, and bubbling over with childish enthusiasm. As they came into my bright, sunny classroom, I could see their little faces turning into frowns, their childish enthusiasm disappearing as if it had been blown away by a hurricane. With my teaching, I aspire for this. The classroom is a place for the learning, the order, and the discipline, not a place for the childish enthusiasm.

Drusilla was always the first to arrive. She sat at her desk, straightened her little skirt, and laced her fingers together with her back erect, and sat patiently waiting for instructions from her beloved teacher. I do adore a child like Drusilla.

She smiled at me. I smiled at her. She nearly levitated out of her chair, such was her happiness at being smiled upon by her beloved teacher.

"Mrs. Ravenbach?"

"Yes, Drusilla?"

"Is something the matter, Mrs. Ravenbach?"

By now the classroom was nearly full. My students are quite punctual. Fear will do that for a child and the parents of that child.

"Yes, Drusilla. I read something which made me quite sad."

"Oh. That's awful."

"So it is."

The other children, they asked all kinds of questions about what had made their beloved Mrs. Ravenbach sad. I was not answering the questions. Private business is private business, but it proved impossible to hold my sadness inside where no one could see it.

"Oh, Mrs. Ravenbach," said Drusilla, "isn't there *anything* we could do to make you feel better?"

They all added their high-voiced two cents. "Pleeeeeease."

"Mrs. Ravenbach, please?!"

"Oh, please."

"What, what, what, what can we do for you?"

To answer *that* question, it did not take me long.

I said, "Wellllllll . . ."

Instantly they understood my meaning. It was a school for gifted and clever children, after all. Together, they all shouted, "Reward Time!"

One of the happiest times for any child in Mrs. Ravenbach's fourth grade classroom is the Reward Time. When the child has done exceedingly well, she or he, although I must confess it is most often a she, gets a reward. The Highest Honor. The two highest honors a child can receive in the classroom of Mrs. Ravenbach are the brushing of the hair and the massaging of the feet.

At Reward Time, the children wait in a perfectly straight line, giddy at the anticipation of the possibility of being allowed to brush my hair using my great-great-grandmother's sterling silver hairbrushes, mirror, and comb made from the finest silver from the Harz Mountains. The Harz Mountains are a beautiful part of Germany, I'm sure you know. The mirror and hairbrushes have the most beautiful handles, made of antlers from a stag shot by Count Otto von St. Paul, the husband of my great-great-grandmother. On one magnificent day, he shot seven stags, and the most beautiful antlers of the most beautiful of all of the seven stags he had shot that day were used for the handles of my hairbrushes and mirror. Think of that, seven animals taken in one day! What a happy man he must have been, outside his hunting lodge with those seven stags piled up like a still-life painting, dead in a heap, bleeding rich, red blood over the gray granite of Baden-Baden.

I think of that happy tableau every time the little children brush my hair with my beautiful sterling silver hairbrushes, which have boar's hair bristles and are very stiff. The children must work their little arms with great vigor to exert themselves enough to get the bristles through my thick, luxurious blond, blond hair, which, I am quick to point out, I do not dye.

Even though their little arms get very tired, the children, they are delighted to brush my hair for minutes, and minutes, and minutes, and minutes at a time. I love the feeling as the bristles tug through my hair as it gets smoother, more glossy, and more gleaming with honey-blond goodness. Good German hair. Good German hairbrushes.

And, of course, attractive high-heel shoes. My Christian Louboutin shoes have a stiletto heel and are the most supple leather imaginable. But even in my beautifully constructed French high-heel designer shoes, my poor feet get tired and sweaty and the bunions and the corns ache and give me enormous trouble. For this reason I have special oils and unguents that the children can apply to my sweaty feet, and rub them, and rub them, and rub them until they do not hurt me anymore. Again, the children fight to get in line for this honor. My homeroom is such a pleasant place, what with the brushing of the hair, the massaging of the feet, and the singing of the *Wehrmacht* marching songs.

I said to Drusilla, "I must confess, a vigorous brushing of the hair might do wonders to improve my sad, sad mood." When I said this, Tobias Wilcox was busy scratching his bottom and did not notice I was giving him a *look*.

I knew precisely what Drusilla would say.

"Oh, Mrs. Ravenbach, I would love to brush your hair! Would that be all right with you?" The other children squirmed in their chairs. They did not enjoy the honor of brushing my hair quite as much as Drusilla.

"Drusilla, please go and retrieve my sterling silver hairbrushes and mirror and comb from their comfy spot in the back of the classroom."

I would not brush Mrs. Ravenbach's
nasty barb wire dyed blonde hair or
massage her stinky pukey feet if she
asked me pretty pretty please with sugar
on top every single day, twice a day
for 17,000,000,000,000,000,000,000,
000,000,000,000,000,000,000,000,
000,000,000,000,000,000 years!!
No. Wait. Make that 17,000,000,000,000,
000,000,000,000,000,000,000,000,000,
000,000,000,000,000,000,000,000,000,
000,000,000,000,000,000,000,000,000,
000,000,000,000,000,000,000,000,000,
000,000,000,000,000,000,000,000,
PLUS INFINITY! YEAH!!! LIGHT YEARS!

"Yes, Mrs. Ravenbach. I'd be delighted," said Drusilla. I loved her so much. Because she loved her teacher.

She hurried to the gold-trimmed red velvet cushion that my sterling silver hairbrushes and mirror and comb rested on.

First Drusilla, then Arthur, then Rachel and Larry and Lisbet and James brushed my hair. With each stroke of the sterling silver hairbrushes, accompanied by spirited grunting by the children from the effort, I felt my mood brighten and the dark, burning, pus-filled carbuncle on my soul began to dissolve away.

After an hour of hair brushing, I felt a good deal better.

And I know the children did too. Because their teacher was no longer sad.

Young Tobias Wilcox had a long face and pouty mouth. It was very clear he desperately wanted to be invited to participate in the Reward Time. I denied him that pleasure. It would not do for him to be enjoying the happiness of making me feel better when he was the cause for my sadness.

From the grumpy look on his unpleasant little face, I could see that, as some might say, young Tobias Wilcox "needed some schoolin'." I resolved to be the one who gave it. In great, industrial-size dollops.

"Come children. Gather round your beloved teacher. It is time for a sing-along!" The children, they squealed with the delight. It was a red-letter day! Reward Time *and* a sing-along! I suppose life for a fourth-grader *could* get better, but I frankly have no idea how. "Fourth-graders, let's sing at the top of our little fourth grade lungs!" I saw Tobias Wilcox smiling. He always enjoyed singing. Well, not for long.

"There once was a teacher . . ."

"THERE ONCE WAS A TEACHER..."

"With blond hair and a wonderful smile..."

"WITH BLOND HAIR AND A WONDERFUL SMILE..."

"She made her students happy..."

"SHE MADE HER STUDENTS HAPPY..."

"Brushing her hair for mile after mile..."

"BRUSHING HER HAIR FOR MILE AFTER MILE..."

"But there was one . . ." I could see Tobias getting a tad anxious.

"BUT THERE WAS ONE..."

"Who didn't behave great..."

"WHO DIDN'T BEHAVE GREAT . . ." Fourth-graders adore a sing-along.

"And wasn't allowed..."

"AND WASN'T ALLOWED..."

"To participate!"

"TO PARTICIPATE!"

At this point, I pointed, ha-ha, get it, at the fat-cheeked clod to my right.

"Toby, Toby, Toby!"

"TOBY, TOBY, TOBY!"

"Wants to go his own way!"

"WANTS TO GO HIS OWN WAY!"

"Like he's pursued by a pack of hounds!"

"LIKE HE'S PURSUED BY A PACK OF HOUNDS!"

"His own way! His own way! His own way!"

"HIS OWN WAY! HIS OWN WAY! HIS OWN WAY!"

"When in fact . . ." Time for the strong finish.

"WHEN IN FACT!"

"He's penitentiary-bound!"

"HE'S PENITENTIARY-BOUND!"

"Toby, Toby, Toby!"

"TOBY, TOBY, TOBY!"

"Come back to the fold!"

"COME BACK TO THE FOLD!"

"Or...be left out...in the cold!" I was regarding him directly. Not a kind regard, either.

"OR...BE LEFT OUT...IN THE COLD!"

The other children, other than Richard, having moved several feet away from him, young Tobias Wilcox stood rigid, hands behind his back, shaking. Bitter, salty tears were running down his chubby little cheeks.

Toby was not having a very wonderful day. Well, it was his own fault.

CHAPTER 7

One beautiful Wednesday morning, I was seated at my beautiful Biedermeier desk in my beautiful, peaceful, quiet classroom. I would even go so far as to say it was a wonderful Wednesday morning. It was early. The first bell had not yet rung.

I heard a small set of footsteps coming timidly down the hall. An excellent teacher recognizes the sound of each child's individual footsteps. Precisely like their handwriting, or a fingerprint. It was young Tobias Wilcox coming down the hall, one miserable step at a time.

He brought his little overweight self quite slowly to the doorway.

Tobias Wilcox leaned into the classroom and said in a quavering voice, "Mrs. Ravenbach?"

"That is my name, Tobias. Are you here early because you are excited because Mr. Grossinger will come today to give his demonstration of the fingerprinting?"

"Sure. But. Can I talk to you?"

"*May* I talk to you?"

"May I talk to you?"

"Of course you may. That is what I am here for, to listen to your every question, no matter how stupid it might be."

"I don't think this's a stupid question."

"No, Tobias, you never do, do you?"

He was shifting from foot to foot, like he needed a potty break.

"Can I ask you a favor?"

"*May* I ask you a favor?"

"May I ask you a favor?" I swear to you, I saw that boy sneer at me.

"Perhaps."

"Can you please be nice to me?"

I wasn't certain I had heard him correctly. I have *never* had a student ask me to be nice to them. Every teacher is always nice to every student all of the time, without fail. Especially a teacher who got her training in East Germany.

I said, "Excuse me?" And I waited. And waited. And I waited some more.

"Well. It's. Like this." He was taking far, far too long to say anything. It was getting a little aggravating. The other students would be arriving and I would need to devote my energy to them and their particular problems, instead of whatever ridiculous idea young Tobias Wilcox had in his mind that I needed to be *nice* to him about. Can you imagine? *Nice*? Such a silly concept.

I stared at the boy. I pride myself on my stare. It is one of my finest skills. I practice it often in the mirror, and on the cat.

His little eyes were brimming with the tears. It's a wonder the

Americans won the war at all. "I was hoping, you might, be able to, be nicer to me . . . cause . . . all this . . . stuff upsets my parents. I don't want to upset my mom and dad. I love them a lot. They do pretty much everything they can for me, and I don't want them to be unhappy."

"Well. Tobias. I merely react to the things that the students are doing. If you feel I am not being, as you say, 'nice,' perhaps there is some little thing inside yourself that is lacking."

"I don't think so."

"Did I ask you what you thought?"

"No, ma'am."

"Well, then."

There was a long pause that was extremely difficult for young Tobias and extremely delicious for me. I must tell you that, so far, this was the High Point of my semester!

"It's important I tell you what I think. I saw it on TV."

"I am certain that you are watching entirely too much television. All American children do this. It is one of the great faults in American parenting."

"I don't think I watch too much TV, but I really need you to know this can't go on."

"Why ever not?"

"Because I can't stand to see my mommy and daddy so upset. My mommy cries herself to sleep at night, at least that's what my daddy says when he makes me breakfast in the morning."

I sat up straight at my desk. When I am sitting up straight, I am very tall. This was getting to be an even *higher* High Point!

"Approach my desk." He did. "Young Tobias?"

"Yes, ma'am?"

"Do you wish to repeat the fourth grade?"

"Excuse me?"

"There is nothing wrong with your hearing, is there?"

"No, ma'am. I hear really good."

"Really well."

"Yes, ma'am. Really well."

"So what was it that I said?"

"You said something about school."

"Yes. I did. And what was it that I said about the school?"

"I don't know."

"Even though you hear well, you don't have a tendency to *listen* terribly well, do you?"

"I think I listen pretty good. Well. For a kid, I mean."

"And what if I told you I did not think you listened so very well?"

"You're the teacher."

"Are you being insolent?"

"No, ma'am."

"Are you aware that you are dangerously close to repeating the fourth grade?"

"How close is 'dangerously close'?"

"Do you know how it is when you are picking a scab, and you pull it off of your skinned-up knee, and you look at it in a bright light and you can see the light shining through it?"

"I know all about picking scabs."

"You are as dangerously close to repeating the fourth grade as that scab is thin."

Did I mention he was sweating?

His breaths came in short, ugly little gulps. It did not sound remotely attractive. There was very little about young Tobias Wilcox that I found attractive.

I leaned down. My nose nearly touched his own, which I am certain he had recently been picking. "Do you have a plan, young Tobias, to ensure that you do not enjoy the fourth grade for a second time?"

"I'm gonna study harder. I'll make better grades. I'll be more organized," he said. Up my back, I got a *Schauer.* The order and the discipline!

"Tell us of your plans for becoming 'better organized.'"

"I'll update my notebook every day. That's what Clarinda Templeton does."

Seeing my smiling face so close to his own, mere inches away, would give him the boost of confidence he needed to come up with the correct answer. It often worked with girls. "Is there anything else?"

"Please don't make me repeat fourth grade."

"Whatever makes you think *I* would *make* you repeat the fourth grade?"

"You're doing all this stuff to me. It's your idea. It's not my idea. I don't wanna repeat fourth grade. School's real expensive. You want me to repeat fourth grade."

"I most certainly do not have any desire for you to repeat the fourth grade. I hope you get your little *Kiste* out of my class as quickly as possible."

"Then why are you being so mean to me?"

"In all my years of teaching, that's the most preposterous thing I've ever heard a little boy say."

"What does 'preposterous' mean?"

"Never you mind. If you want to be repeating the fourth grade, you will do the things that are necessary for you to repeat the fourth grade. If you do not wish to be repeating the fourth grade, you will do the things that are necessary to keep yourself from repeating the fourth grade. The only person who has ever repeated the fourth grade in all my years of teaching at the McKegway School for Clever and Gifted Children was Fast Eddie LeJeune. He repeated the fourth grade, and, as every child I ever teach knows, he is currently in a federal correctional facility serving richly deserved hard time."

I could see his fat little chin quivering. At any moment he was likely to burst into great big fat tears. What a High Point *that* would be for Mrs. Ravenbach! Something wonderful that night to share with Mr. Ravenbach over several generous glasses of Assmannshauser Hollenberg Spatburgunder Spätlese Trocken wine with fresh Floured Board bread and country *pâté*.

I gave him a tissue from my desk. The students are always so honored when I give them a tissue from my rhinestone-encrusted tissue box. He used it to blow his snotty nose. I indicated the trash can. He properly disposed of the heavy tissue.

"I *can't* come back to fourth grade next year. There's no way I'd survive it. Please don't make me! I can't sleep. This's killing me."

I sniffed. "I carefully designed the curriculum so any typical fourth grade child can prosper while studying the course material. You are certainly a typical fourth grade child. Believe me. I have seen plenty."

I smiled at him. As far as I was concerned, I had answered his question and our discussion was at an end. I smiled again and

cracked my knuckles. The *craaaaaaaack* was incredibly satisfying and made him flinch.

That, too, was satisfying. To me.

He looked at me a long while. He was thinking something.

Then he smiled.

His smile was not terribly friendly.

Not friendly at all.

I had a feeling that, behind his eyeballs, deep in his little-boy
brain, I could see old-fashioned gears turning and steam-powered
pistons spinning heavy flywheels round and round and round.
He *was* thinking *something*.

He said in a calm, pleasant tone, "Thank you, Mrs. Ravenbach, for being so kind and warm and understanding. Thank you
so much."

What a clever child. It was heartwarming that young Tobias
Wilcox and I had been able to reach an understanding. An excellent and caring teacher can always reach an understanding with
her students. A high, high, high High Point!

He waddled over and sat his fat little bottom at his desk, lifted
the lid, and hid behind it until the rest of the children arrived and
we began our schooling.

MY FANTASTIC CLEVER WELL THOUGHT OUT UNABLE-TO-BE DETECTED SUPREME ALLIED COMMANDERS AGENTS OF S·H·I·E·L·D PLAN OF ALL PLANS

WAYS TO DO HER IN!

1.) tie her to an anthill and pour honey on her
2.) tie her to a cannon and say "Sayonara!"
3.) give her pretend candy that expands in her stomach
4.) give her pretend candy that explodes in her stomach!
5.) make her watch "It's a Wonderful Life" until her eyes bleed
6.) email Carleton for great ideas

Resolved. Tell Drusie she's nice. Even if she's the Teeeeecher's Pet. Any girl whose hair smells like grass that's just got cut has to be okay. Doesn't she?

Sigh.

CHAPTER 8

It was with great anticipation that I journeyed outside to the playground. For several days, I had not had the opportunity to watch the children doing their running, owing to the heavy workload of grading little papers, reading little homeworks, attending to the little children and their little tiny problems.

Young Tobias Wilcox, however, was not a tiny problem. He was, in fact, a problem the size of the *Graf Zeppelin*. If you are not knowing what the *Graf Zeppelin* was, look it up in the World Book Encyclopedia at your school library. That is what the encyclopedia is for, for young children to look things up in. The Internet is a stupid way to look up something, if you have an encyclopedia.

It was with *Zeppelin*-size anticipation, yes, that I sat down at my preferred spot in the center of the playground and began the eavesdropping. Sitting on my elegant collapsible leather hiking stick/chair doing my knitting, I was able to hear clearly what the children were saying. After reading a private journal, the eavesdropping is the next best thing for peering into a child's innermost thoughts, which makes the teaching experience so much more rich and profound.

It is always amazing to me how little children have no concept of how good a teacher's hearing might possibly be.

Tobias Wilcox was running with his friend Richard Kaliski, doing out-loud internal musing. That kind of distracted, disorganized thinking is much like the doodles I saw on many pages in his journal. Anyone who doodles is unquestionably an intellectual lightweight. All teachers know this. It is a grand source of amusement and joy in the teachers' lounge when the teachers come in and show off their students' most recent doodles and laugh at them, knowing the children will never turn out well.

No child who doodled ever became a heart surgeon.

Through clever control and discipline, I was able to keep my antique ivory knitting needles from making a sound, and quite easily could make out what young Tobias Wilcox was saying to bald-headed Richard Kaliski. They were huffing and puffing a great deal. It sounded as if Richard was on the verge of a massive heart attack.

After an asinine, time-wasting discussion of Richard's fervent desire to have his own iPod, which was doomed to failure because of a lack of available financing, Tobias said, "Want to come over on Saturday and work on Sub Club stuff?"

"Can we listen to the game?"

"Zip Tuggle rocks!"

"Baseball rocks!"

They did that stupid fist-bump thing, and then I heard Tobias say, "Do you think Fast Eddie LeJeune's still alive?"

Oh, my.

"Good question. Want a Tootsie Roll?"

"If he's not dead, where do you think he's in prison?"

"Why you wanna know about Fast Eddie LeJeune?"

"She hated him. She hates me."

"Worse than Arthur's parents hate each other, if that's at all possible. Wonder why."

"Cause she's stupid. You're smart. You like me. She should too."

Richard grunted in agreement. At least it sounded like a grunt. It may have been a stab of paralyzing pain in his left arm—the first step before a heart attack. That would have been a better story to tell in the teachers' lounge than about the doodling: "At the recess today, my student dropped dead from a myocardial infarction. Too much cheese pizza."

Tobias said, "Do you think there's really a Mr. Ravenbach?"

"Why wouldn't there be?"

"Who'd marry someone as mean as her?"

"Excellent point you make, young sir."

I nearly got up and jammed my antique ivory knitting needles into that little boy's eyes.

Tobias and Richard caught up to Arthur Hester, who stumbled along like a broken half-track. The three of them started talking about submarines and I started listening to a different, vastly more interesting conversation between two fourth grade girls about their parents' problems with *their* parents, but Tobias's brief exchange with Richard did not soon leave my mind.

I was shocked, dismayed, and appalled at the thought that young Tobias Wilcox was uttering the name Fast Eddie LeJeune to his dimpled-knee chum Richard. Everyone knows that the recess running is a sacred ritual and why would anyone, any student, any human being defile a sacred ritual with the mention of Fast Eddie LeJeune?

Had he but asked, I could have told Tobias with great precision where Fast Eddie LeJeune was to be found. Germans invented the precision. Fast Eddie LeJeune was, and Tobias would have known this had he ever paid attention in class, in a stone-walled building with abominable food, unsanitary bathing facilities, and highly unpleasant companionship every day for the rest of his life. Not unlike living in France.

Ha-ha, my little joke.

I abandoned my listening post just before the recess came to an end. It was a successful recess, to be sure. Plenty of running. But only four children threw up. Always room for the improvement!

In class that afternoon, Mr. Grossinger was our special guest. He worked for the district attorney's office. He was a fingerprint expert. On his head he had little white hairs that poked out in all sorts of funny directions. He had little, tiny, round glasses and little, tiny, slit eyes that belonged in a pig. I mean no harm when I say that, as it is just the truth, which Mrs. Ravenbach always, always tells.

As he gave his fascinating lecture on the fingerprinting, Mr. Grossinger explained about inking the plate and inking the finger by rotating the hand from the easy to the awkward position. This keeps the fingers relaxed so they may be lifted from the card without smudging or blurring the fingerprints. He was so exact. I do appreciate exactness.

Mr. Grossinger had a lovely smile.

The little children liked the fingerprint expert more than

possibly I could have imagined. The fingerprint expert was the funniest person to come in my classroom in many a long time and the children, they loved him enormously. He was terribly jovial, waving wanted posters of real criminals and putting them up beside each child's face and saying, "Are you wanted for extortion?!" "You look like you might be on the lam for armed robbery!" and other amusing things like that.

What the children liked the most, of course, was the inking of the fingers and the rolling of the fingers on the paper and generally making a gigantic mess all over everywhere, including much laughing by yours truly, Mrs. Ravenbach, who, I am quite emphatic to say, had *never* been fingerprinted in her life.

For some unknown reason that day, Tobias was superbly attentive.

Each little child lined up in a row and Mr. Grossinger took their little hand in his enormous, firm hand and rolled their fingers on the inked glass and then carefully rolled their fingers on the fingerprint paper. He was very precise, almost like a German.

Tobias Wilcox and Richard Kaliski and Arthur Hester nudged each other and chatterboxed and asked many questions, most of which were not terribly stupid for a change. I was delighted they were perhaps at last taking an interest in *something* besides submarines.

When it was time to fingerprint Mrs. Ravenbach, Mr. Grossinger took my hand gently in his large and strong hand, and I could feel the warmth as he held my hand in his and the soft look in his eyes as he gazed upon me, and gently squeezed my fingers one by one, rolling them in the warm ink and on the warm paper in the sunshiny classroom.

Report on Mr. Grossinger, our class visitor

by Toby Wilcox

Fingerprinting is cool. Mr. Grossinger the fingerprint expert came to class today and brought his fingerprinting kit. The parts of a latent fingerprinting kit are:

Black powder
Black magnetic powder
Fluorescent blue magnetic powder
Fluorescent orange magnetic powder
Frosted Lifting Tape Powder
2" Clear Lifting Tape
Mini Scalpel Cutter
Bottle Rough Lift
Fiber Brushes
Feather Brush
Magnetic Applicator
White Lifting Cards
Black Lifting Cards
UV Lamp

Neat—o! Can the Sub Club use a fingerprint expert? Ask Richard!

A History of Fingerprinting

Fingerprinting began long, long ago. In ancient Babylon, fingerprints were used as signatures. As early as King Hammurabi, in 1792 BCE, the good guys would take fingerprints of people who had been arrested. In 1788, a German guy, Johann Christope Andreas Mayer, discovered that fingerprints were unique to people. In 1902, the first person was identified, arrested, and convicted on the basis of fingerprint evidence. Many bad guys wear gloves to keep from leaving fingerprints. But, sometimes, the gloves can leave

There is nothing like the tender handling by a government employee.

Mr. Grossinger told several witty stories about pursuing bank robbers, car thieves, and a woman who stole a white angora sweater, all imprisoned because of the fingerprinting. Mr. Grossinger was quite the superb storyteller. I do like a jolly man. They liven up the house after dinner. Had there not been a Mr. Ravenbach waiting for me at home, perhaps I might have given Mr. Grossinger my telephone number.

When Mr. Grossinger had departed, amid great applause and peals of laughter and smiles and friendly waves from the children, I handed each child their fingerprint sheets.

Everyone had one except me. How very odd.

I am quite certain Mr. Grossinger took it with him, perhaps as a tender souvenir of our pleasant afternoon together.

CHAPTER 9

It is of paramount importance that each and every child do all of his or her homework every day. If they are not keeping up with their homework every day, they will become stragglers. And eventually, stragglers will have to be shot.

Ha-ha. A little joke that amuses me.

I'm sure you understand, something not even slightly amusing, and far, far worse than being a straggler, is being a liar.

Young Tobias Wilcox was always a forgetful child. He would have his book, he would not have his book. He would leave his gym clothes at his home. He would forget to have them washed. He would forget his sneakers. He would remember his sneakers but forget the gym clothes. He would forget what his homework assignment was. He would complete his homework during the study hall, take it home with him (despite my wisely suggesting he leave it in his desk), and then he would, of course, forget it at home and not bring it to school the next day. He was an amazing child for the forgetfulness. He *invented* new ways of forgetting things. Tobias Wilcox was the Albert Einstein of forgetting his things!

On this particular day, we were studying the science. The science is beautiful because it is precise. But the science will not work unless the student has done the night before his or her reading at home. No work at home, no learning in the classroom, and I become vexed.

I had come into class early, as is my nature. To be punctual is to be before time, not on time. Any idiot knows that. As I was tidying up, I checked in every student's desk. It is important to know what is going on in their little lives and to see what perhaps they might be hiding.

In Tobias's desk I found his science book. The little forgetful child had forgotten his science book. This means the reading the night before he could not possibly have done. No work at home, no learning in the classroom. Indeed, I was *quite* vexed.

When it became time for the science class, I asked Tobias about his homework. He said he had done the reading.

Behind my great, round bosom, my heart nearly flip-flopped to a stop.

I regarded that little boy from high above him with my strong, German eyes, and I said, "You have *not*."

I was surprised at how his eyes were able to meet mine. Most children look away when Mrs. Ravenbach gives them even her most friendly look, and this look was not that look.

"I did the reading," said Tobias.

Every small face in the classroom was watching me with great anticipation.

I said, "*You. Are. A. Liar.*"

Did he cry? He did not.

Did he admit that he was a liar? He did not.

Did he shake and tremble and prostrate himself before me? No, the wretched little child did not do any of these things.

With great impudence he said, "I am not a liar, Mrs. Ravenbach. I did my reading."

I told the impertinent child to open up his desk. He did so. I said, "What is in your desk?"

He said as he rummaged, "Well, a bunch of paper, my baseball glove, a ruler, a pencil box, Pokémon cards, more paper, a Tech Deck, a stink bomb, Silly Putty, a rubber band ball, two packs of Big League Chew, more paper, and a design I made for my Halloween costume as Frankenstein."

I said, "What *books* are in there, young Tobias?"

"My poetry book, a book about Danny Dunn and anti-gravity paint, and my science book."

Well, then, the entire class knew, of course, the child was not telling the truth.

I spoke to him as kindly as I could. "Tobias, I want you to write a letter to your parents. I want you to tell them how you have lied to your teacher and to your classmates, and that you could not possibly have done your homework because your science book has been here in your desk *all the night long.*"

He protested even more, saying, "But Mrs. Ravenbach, I did my homework. I read the reading. I promise you, I did."

I said, "This conversation, we have finished. Do not continue to lie to me any further. Write the letter to your parents, have them sign it, bring it to me tomorrow, and I will show it to the class and Principal Hertenstein. And then we shall see what we shall see."

Every child in the classroom was giving young Tobias Wilcox

a look of "you are a stupid-faced liar." Except Richard Kaliski and Arthur Hester. They were terrified for their friend.

"Call my parents. They'll tell you."

"I do not need to call your parents. I know you are lying."

"You don't believe me?"

"I do not."

"You don't believe me even when I'm telling the truth."

"You are not."

"*That's. What. You. Think!*"

Every single child, with the exception of bald-headed Richard Kaliski, gasped. The classroom had a feeling, a wave, a current coursing through it like an electric eel. I sensed rebellion.

I was in grave danger of losing *control,* the iron-clad, hot-riveted control I had patiently constructed hour by hour, day by day, week by week since that first class back in the hot, sweaty days of August.

And now this.

Only the thought of my fifth Golden Apple award for Excellence in Teaching kept me from falling on the floor and having a conniption fit.

That little boy! His dirty cheeks. His filthy hat. His bumpy little teeth. His nasty little tone of voice, his nasty little face. Something inside me reached a breaking point. My fear for his classmates, running wild without the order and the discipline, boiled over . . . *all* of them would end in the penitentiary!

I had had enough of this contrary child who did not have enough sense to know when his teacher had his best interest at heart. I reached for him, my hand outstretched, my bright red fingernails shaking with feeling, about to grab him by his filthy dirty collar—with a crystal-clear vision of what would happen next . . .

What would happen next would be the dragging of the child to Principal Hertenstein's office. There would be the tears. The sobbing. The evidence. Followed by many more tears and then, triumphantly, the truth.

And the truth would be followed by . . . the *expulsion*!

Tobias Wilcox would be expelled from the McKegway School for Clever and Gifted Children!

Heaped in shame, he would drag his torn and dirty book bag across the school parking lot and get into the cheap automobile of his mortally embarrassed mother—while the entire student body of the McKegway School for Clever and Gifted Children jeered at him and threw the spit wads.

To lie to a teacher is a terribly poor idea. The child will always be caught. To lie to Mrs. Leni Ravenbach is a very terribly poor idea. The child will always be expelled.

These delicious thoughts were racing through my over-heated but beautiful brain as I reached for the child's grape jelly–encrusted shirt—

The little wretch said, in the calmest tone of voice you can possibly imagine . . . "Mrs. Ravenbach?" He said it so sweetly, it was as if little birds were singing.

All of the students, with the possible exception of Sykes Granberry, who was, no doubt scratching his bottom, became perfectly silent. So perfectly silent that I imagined I heard, as young Tobias Wilcox was smiling up at me, his teeth perfectly white—I noticed for the first time, he did have beautiful teeth—I thought I saw a tiny bright white star shimmer off one of his front teeth, accompanied by the tiniest *ping!* of a glockenspiel. It seemed so real that I momentarily forgot where I was and I barely heard the loathsome child say, "Mrs. Ravenbach . . . why don't you look in my backpack?"

Everyone was holding their breath.

I unzipped the backpack of Tobias Wilcox. Reached into the festering interior. Closed my elegant fingers around something hard, rectangular, and gummy. From the dark recesses of his dirty backpack, I removed . . . *a science book*!

He said, "Pretty neat, hunh?"

Awash in a dark, deep, ghastly sinking feeling, I could tell the children were all on the verge of rebelling. I could see it rolling up from their toes to their bellies and a huge explosion was about to come flooding into the classroom like a tidal wave of disorder and anti-discipline.

This was about to be a disaster.

The students were about to *laugh*.

I stopped it before it started.

I smiled at Tobias.

My *most* charming smile. The students had not seen my *most* charming smile in weeks, and as they had *never* seen it directed at young Tobias Wilcox, such was their fascination at this unexpected event, the awful laugh died before it could be born. *Wunderbar*!

"Well done, young lad. It appears you have two science books. One for the school and one for the home. What a *clever* young fellow you are."

"Remember you said I needed to be less forgetful? I knew I could never be less forgetful, and I know science is a big deal, so I got my mom to get me another book, which cost a lot of money, but I didn't wanna worry about being forgetful. Sweet, hunh?"

He smiled again. A smile of nasty victory. On his little front tooth, again glittered that twirling little bright star. *Ping!*

It was difficult for Mrs. Ravenbach to breathe, as if every ounce of air had rushed out of the room—like a bunch of cheap carpet salesmen leaving in a hurry when, next door, they pour the free beer. I found just enough breath down in my great, massive, strong-as-leather lungs to barely announce, "Recess!"

Mrs. Ravenbach is a ~~███████~~
~~███ ████ █████ ██████~~
~~█████ █████ ████████~~
~~████████ ███ █ ████ ███~~
~~█████ ███ ███ █ ████~~
~~███ ███ █████ ████ ███~~
~~████ ███ █████ ████ ███~~
~~█ ████ █ ██████ ████ ███~~
~~███ ███ ██████ ████ ████~~
~~██████████ ███ ███ ██~~
~~██ █████ █████ ████ ██~~
~~███ ███ █████ ███ ███~~
~~████ ████ ████████~~ It's time
to be more careful.

That evening, I was so very lucky that my dear friend, Mrs. Button, was at home. She answered my telephone call and came over straightaway. What a blessing!

I was so upset by the near rebellion caused by young Tobias Wilcox that Mrs. Button had to make the tea. Her little figure bustling back and forth across my kitchen with such industry and animation calmed me greatly, I can assure you.

We sat in my beautifully appointed living room, enjoying tea and sweet cakes. I sipped from my delicate Meissen cup and my breathing slowly returned to a normal pace. Finally, Mrs. Button sensed, in her most delicate way, that I was able at last to approach the terrible situation which had precipitated my calling her to my aid. She was so deeply interested in the comings and goings of the schoolchildren.

"Leni, Leni, my dear Leni. What possibly could have happened at school today to upset you so, so greatly? There's not a problem with the football team?"

"No. No. It was . . . It was . . ." I was unable to pronounce the words.

"Toby Wilcox. Something should be done about him. Beastly child."

"It was awful, awful."

"I trust in your hour of distress Mr. Ravenbach was a stalwart companion."

"As always, as always. He says to thank you for coming over. Out for the moment, he is buying apples and other strudel ingredients. Mr. Ravenbach is happy to shop for me, as he does love his strudel."

"Would that Mr. Button were such a helpful helpmate. He's

good at tying fishing flies and complaining." She sighed and took a careful breath. "Leni. It is not my place to give advice. But, as a Wilcox family neighbor, I believe I have some insight into their situation that might be helpful to you."

"My dear Mrs. Button, there's nothing I would treasure more than to be given advice from you, my wise and caring friend."

My dear friend's little rodent-like face positively shone with excitement. Her shapeless dress quivered on her tiny-boned form like a sail in a breeze as her little body nearly shook with the enjoyment of what she then said. Her voice, I remember, was a wee bit . . . scary. Her tone, I remember, was deliciously . . . controlling.

She said, "Sometimes, Leni, darling, you just have to show children what's what." The simple wisdom of her statement was overwhelming. "You must endeavor to get him to . . . *appreciate* the situation."

While I sipped my tea, I began to think.

Tea is so useful for the thinking, don't you agree?

CHAPTER 10

Sitting at my gorgeous Biedermeier desk, knitting a lovely lavender scarf for Mr. Ravenbach, admiring the three loaves of Floured Board farm bread and gift certificates to Trumilou and the Ritz Café, the finest restaurants in the city, which were laid neatly on my desk, I moved my gaze to my pupils, who were all working on a mathematics assignment. Which one would be able to help me to help young Tobias Wilcox in his journey through life? Which one might be the most useful?

Which one might be willing to betray a classmate ... ?

It was, at that point, that Dame Fortune smiled on me. When you are a wonderful person, wonderful things fall into your lap.

Children love the potty words. They hear their parents using such language and, because they want to be big like their parents, they are using the potty words. Whenever they think a grown-up is not listening, it is the potty words, the potty words, the potty words, here, there, and everywhere.

But the children, they are not always realizing when a

grown-up is listening. Even a child as bright and clever as bald-headed Richard Kaliski.

I heard a pencil roll across a desk.

I heard a hand scrape for it.

I heard the pencil fall to the floor.

I heard the point break.

I heard a little boy's voice say, "Oh, crap."

My great blond-haired head rotated like a dish antenna on a *Narvik* class destroyer.

And to my delight, I saw him. Little bald-headed Richard Kaliski, his face so perfectly round, and white, and soft. If I had poked my thumbs into bread dough, that would have been his face.

From across the room, like a shining spotlight, his white face was staring at me in utter fright. I nodded to him. To let him know that I knew. Then I continued my knitting. I was taking no steps at that precise moment, of course. Better to let the child dread the coming annihilation. For hours.

Later that day, when the bell rang for the children to go to the recess, I crooked my finger at Richard Kaliski. What a sweatbox he was! I felt that if you turned the heat up on him, he would melt and puddle on the floor into a big sticky ball of grease, wearing short pants. Dirty short pants.

While filing out, the children watched Richard slink to my desk with his eyes cast down, each child assuming Richard was about to be guillotined. Of course nothing could be further from the case, but that is what the little children sometimes think. Should I tell them something different?

Mother. Father. Teacher. God.

"Richard?"

"Yes, Mrs. Ravenbach?"

"What word did I hear you using earlier in the day?"

"I don't know."

Children! Do they think you are deaf, dumb, blind, and retarded? "Did you say a mud puddle word?"

"No, ma'am. Mrs. Ravenbach, ma'am."

"I heard you." He stood there sweating. How unattractive. "What . . . word . . . did . . . you . . . say?"

I have a wonderful Bavarian cuckoo clock in my classroom. Its loud, brittle ticking was the perfect accompaniment to his growing terror. At last, *natürlich*, he cracked.

His voice was as miniature as a leprechaun through the wrong end of a telescope. "I said 'crap.'"

"Is the mud puddle word you used a word you would like me to relay to your parents?" He shook his pathetic bald head. I took great pleasure in noticing he was right on the edge of the tears. "It is a fact, is it not, young Richard, that you adore your teacher, Mrs. Ravenbach, more than anything in the world?"

He nodded.

"And for your favorite teacher is it not true that you would do anything in the world?"

He nodded.

"Here is what I am wanting you to do. For the betterment of the McKegway School for Clever and Gifted Children."

"I'm always happy to help the school, Mrs. Ravenbach."

I said, "Richard. Are you familiar with the expression 'mole'?"

"Yes, ma'am. You've got a big, hairy one, right on your chin."

This was not the appropriate moment for me to make a fist

and knock him on his *Kiste*. "No. Not that kind of mole." Richard, his bald round head staring up at me, shiny in the afternoon light, blinked his big, wet eyes. Richard *was* the most intelligent child in the class. "For the running of the classroom, it is very important for the teacher to understand what is going on with every single one of her beloved students."

I looked down at him. I am very tall. He said, "What kind of a mole, Mrs. Ravenbach?"

"Someone hidden deep in an organization, someone no one would suspect is feeding important, helpful information to someone outside the organization."

"A spy?"

I smiled. "It might interest you to know that the espionage agents, they are always paid. In cash. Perhaps there are trinkets you wish to buy for yourself for which your parents do not give you enough allowance." He vigorously shook his head. "I need you to tell me what young Tobias Wilcox is thinking. And doing. What little notes he scribbles with his fat little hands in class. Who he talks to. Who he thinks about. And most especially what he thinks about me, his teacher, who he should worship and adore, but who I am afraid . . . sadly, he does not."

"Mrs. Ravenbach, I'd never spy on Toby! You're out of your mind!"

I leaned forward. I put my fingers around his Adam's apple. My thumb on the left side, my first two fingers on the right side, with my sharp fingernails, and I squeezed.

The cuckoo clock ticked and ticked.

When he blinked, I knew I had him.

I told Drusie I thought she was nice.
It felt good to say out loud. Wow, did it.

I gave her one of my best X-Men comic
books. That felt good too.

What I think: She kinda smiled. I
hope.

What I know: She didn't sneer at me.

Yay!

It was a bright and sunny day at the McKegway School for Clever and Gifted Children. As you know, it is *always* a bright and sunny day at the McKegway School for Clever and Gifted Children, especially in the classroom of Mrs. Ravenbach. At parent-teacher conferences, the parents always say to me, they say, "How do you manage to make the children come home so sunny and bright?"

And I always answer, "Because sunniness and a bright mood begin in the heart. When your heart is pure and clean and clear, sun will surround it. The children sense this and are drawn to me, and my happy, upbeat mood, in my sunny and bright classroom."

The parents, they smile and they go on about their important business. Like purchasing me gift certificates from the restaurants I like the most! Ha-ha.

Richard "The Mole" Kaliski . . . he was not so sunny and bright as he delivered information about his friend Tobias, such as what the night before he had for dinner, odd jobs he was doing to earn the extra money, what sin he had committed that his parents were upset about, which homework assignments were proving particularly difficult . . . He did not smile his sunniest smile as he betrayed his friend.

I was feeling a good deal more confident in my ability to help young Tobias Wilcox.

That particular sunny morning we were discussing the careers.

Drusilla asked if she could brush my hair later that afternoon. I, *natürlich,* replied in the affirmative. I do love to have my hair brushed. Doesn't everyone?

After our nourishing luncheon, the bright-eyed children

were eagerly wondering what new and wonderful task I was going to assign them to do. All the fresh, glowing, eager faces! Arthur, Richard, Drusilla, Trevania, and Sophie. That was only in the first row! I do enjoy having a large class, the more children with whom to share my extraordinary knowledge!

I put down my knitting and said, "Class, this afternoon we're all going to write a haiku."

"Are you gonna write one too, Mrs. Ravenbach?"

"No, Tobias. I have had books of poetry published in many languages around the world, so there is no need for me to write a haiku today, just to prove that I know how to do it."

"Oh, sorry," he said, "you said 'we're all.' I musta misunderstood."

"A haiku is a poem. A poem with very strict rules. We Germans are very interested in strict rules."

"I'll say!" said Arthur. It seemed that young Arthur Hester had been taking lessons from young Tobias. Rudeness lessons.

"A haiku consists of three lines, five syllables in line one, seven syllables in line two, and again five syllables in line three. Very simple and wonderfully elegant."

I assigned the children the wonderful exercise of writing a haiku about Vincent van Gogh, the finest painter in the history of the world. It is a pity he was not German. He was Dutch, and being Dutch is very nearly being German.

I know Mr. Ravenbach certainly enjoys having me around the house after I've been looking at van Gogh paintings. He feels I make him a bigger omelet in the morning. I disagree. It is my feeling that I am always giving him a large-size omelet in the mornings, but he feels that, after viewing a painting or two by van Gogh, I am a wee bit more generous around the kitchen.

In any event, van Gogh is my hero. I place him higher than Beethoven, and you know how I feel about Beethoven!

It was a sunny and bright day in my classroom, and the children's little heads were bent over their lined paper, carefully and beautifully writing their haiku about Vincent van Gogh.

Young Tobias Wilcox finished first and was looking around. He always finished his work quickly, with much haste, and a great deal of overall sloppiness.

From my high spot at my teacher's desk, I said, "Tobias?"

"Yes, Mrs. Ravenbach."

"You have finished?"

"Yes, ma'am. It was real easy."

"I have never found writing haiku to be easy. Yet you do, on the first haiku you've ever written?"

"Sure did!"

"Please. Bring it to my desk. I should like to read it."

"Sure thing, Mrs. Ravenbach!" Tobias Wilcox certainly was in a jolly mood. Perhaps he was so proud of his work that he couldn't wait to share it with his beloved teacher.

His grubby little hand thrust a wrinkled piece of paper upon my desk. Small flecks of dirt fell off the paper and soiled the clean, lovely wooden surface of my beautiful teacher's desk. I flicked the dirt toward him and lifted his crinkled paper. It did not take long to read his haiku, nor did it take long to realize that young Mr. Wilcox was doing his best to irritate his beloved teacher. He was generally a success at irritating people.

"Your haiku is this?"

"Yepper!"

Van Gogh drives cars fast
Formula One is his sport
He drives really well

Cool. ♡ Drusie

Van Gogh hits some oil
He spins out of control, oh!
Spinning Spinning skid!

His car smacks the wall!
Pieces scatter everywhere!
Van Gogh breathes his last

Van Gogh can not work
His canvas is slick with snot
Dripping on the floor!

My painting is junk!
Stupid stupid work of art
Hate it hate it, yuk!

I know just how
he feels. D.

It had been a difficult morning. Sophie Taschlin had thrown up in the teachers' lounge while asking for a peppermint to ease her unsettled stomach. We gave her the peppermint. It did not help. Because Sophie existed on a diet solely consisting of the Pop-Tarts, the teachers' lounge had to be evacuated.

I was in no mood to be toyed with by young Tobias Wilcox.

"Would you please read your haiku to the class?"

"Sure thing!" He waddled up to my desk, reached his fat little hand up high, and I shoved the nasty piece of paper into his outstretched grubby little fingers. I could see the dirt under his fingernails.

He unfolded his nasty paper, smoothed it on his grubby, bare knee, stood up as straight as was possible, and read his haiku out loud. I quote, precisely, word for word because it is burned eternally into my memory.

Van Gogh is boring.
Van Gogh is really snoring.
Van Gogh is quite dead.

The little monster looked up at me and smiled. I will go to my grave believing that child woke up every single morning trying to come up with a manner in which to irritate me at some point during the day. I must confess, I lost a little bit of the self-control.

"Why would you write a haiku like *that* about the magnificent painter Vincent van Gogh?!"

"Van Gogh's not magnificent. He's stupid."

"What?! WHAT!!"

"I think you heard me." His tone of voice was the most sarcastic you can possibly imagine. And once you've imagined that, double it. And once you imagine *that,* triple it.

Never in my life as a teacher, as an adult, or even as a person had I felt such hatred for someone four feet tall.

"How can you possibly think van Gogh is stupid?"

"Over spring break, I saw a museum with his stuff. He can't paint, and everything he paints is stupid."

"He is one of the finest painters in the history of Western civilization!"

"Why do you care whether I like him or not? I like Norman Rockwell."

"Van Gogh is an *artist*! Norman Rockwell was an *illustrator*! The two have nothing in common!"

"I disagree."

"You are not allowed to disagree with your teacher! It causes ill will among the other students, and does not follow a clear path toward the order and the discipline!"

"You can't tell me how to think."

"You may not believe that I can tell you how to think, but I guarantee you Principal Hertenstein can!"

If I were not the type of person who maintains herself in peak physical condition at all times, eating well, mostly yogurt and *Müsli*, I might have had a stroke right there at that very moment. Fortunately for me, and for my students, I did not.

Young Tobias gave me a queer little Tobias Wilcox look and said, deliberately, "Maybe you better send me to his office, then."

"An *excellent* plan!"

"What do I tell him why I got sent there?"

"Because you wrote a haiku disrespecting one of the greatest painters in the history of painting, that's why! Now go! *Mach schnell!*"

That child gave me the most devilish smile and said, "Sure thing, Mrs. Ravenbach!"

Late that afternoon, after dismissal, I was feeding a live rat to the python in the glass cage in the corner of my lovely, beautiful, sunny classroom. I do so enjoy watching the python eating the rats. It reminds me of how I sometimes am feeling toward my students. Feeding the live rats to a python is not something you do in front of children, because it upsets them. Not, ha-ha, nearly as much as it upsets the rats.

As the rat was cowering, again reminding me of my pupils, Mr. Hertenstein came in.

Principal Hertenstein rarely came to visit the classroom. Administrators visiting the classroom is not the finest idea. It is best for the administration to do the administrating and the teachers to do the teaching.

Nonetheless, I was honored to have Principal Hertenstein in my classroom. Mr. Hertenstein was a wise and thoughtful man. Perhaps he was of German extraction. He was so attractive in his

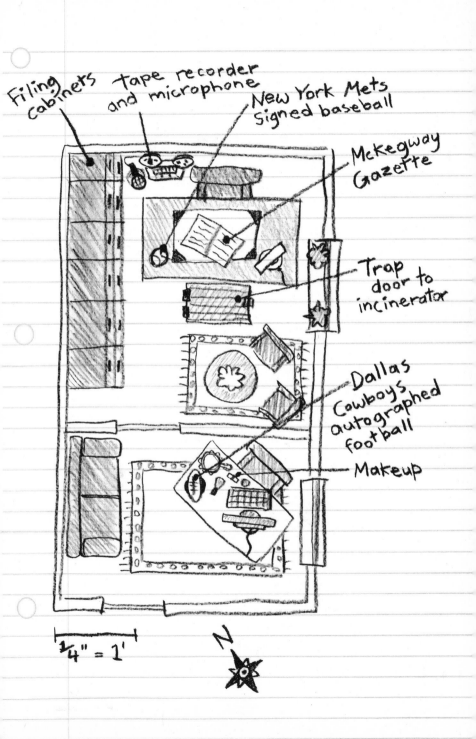

Filing cabinets

tape recorder and microphone

New York Mets Signed baseball

Mckegway Gazette

Trap door to incinerator

Dallas Cowboys autographed football

Makeup

$\frac{1}{4}$" = 1'

N

three-piece suit and polka-dot tie. His gray hair combed just so. The McKegway School for Clever and Gifted Children was so wonderfully lucky to have his firm, guiding hand at the helm. I must confess, that when Principal Hertenstein stood near me, my heart did beat a tiny bit faster.

He only wore the sneakers, which meant one could never hear him coming. This was his special technique to creep up on the misbehaving children. I had often seen children nearly die of fright when Mr. Hertenstein appeared, as if from nowhere behind their backs, and cleared his throat. Their frightened faces truly could make one laugh.

It was not quite as amusing, however, to have him sneak up and suddenly appear in one's own private classroom.

"Mrs. Ravenbach?"

It took quite the effort not to have a stroke. "Yes, Principal Hertenstein?"

"Toby Wilcox was in my office today." There was something in his voice that concerned me, just a wee, tiny little bit. When one's fifth Golden Apple for Excellence in Teaching hangs in the balance, any possible shift in the scales is worth noticing. "He recited his little haiku to me. It did not seem to be worthy of being sent to my office."

Down my back a chill as cold as the beautiful Danube River ran. Could it be that Principal Hertenstein *disagreed* with me, Mrs. Leni Ravenbach? I said, "It was a most disrespectful haiku."

"Your opinion, of course. My concern is my time, and he wasted an enormous amount of it climbing all over my book-cases, rifling through my file cabinets, and generally making a nuisance of himself in my office. While Miss Scott was occupied sorting her bottles of fingernail polish by color, I had to deal with three phone calls from irate parents and had no time to prevent Toby from visiting every corner of my office. I do not like having my time wasted. And I most emphatically do not like little children going through my private office files."

"F-files . . . ?"

"Yes, Mrs. Ravenbach. My files. My personal private executive files. My personal, private, *private* executive files."

The cold Danube River flowing down my spine suddenly began to feel as if fifteen platoons of *Waffen-SS* soldiers had thrown nine tons of ice into it. Each.

"Do you have, Principal Hertenstein, any idea what files he was . . . inspecting?"

"When I dragged him away, he was rooting around in the L.E. drawer."

Now it felt as if the *Waffen-SS* soldiers had dropped *dry* ice into the Danube.

* * *

PRINCIPAL HERTENSTEIN IS MY KIND OF PRINCIPAL IN that he maintains the precision timing. He left for his exercise club every day precisely at 4:15 p.m.. The order and the discipline!

His secretary, Miss Scott, who was a bit of the va-va-voom and not the sort of secretary who makes a correct impression sitting at a desk painting and polishing her fingernails all the day long, always left exactly three minutes after he did. Probably to go to a bar to meet sailors. Which meant, if one waited ten minutes after that, there was no danger of being noticed slipping into the principal's office.

Like an arrow shot from the crossbow, I went straight to his personal, private, executive files. In the drawer marked *L.E.*, I could see one file sticking up and smudged, as if it had been grabbed by fat, dirty fingers on a fat, dirty hand.

A file marked "LeJeune, Edward T."

I could feel the beautiful Danube beginning to freeze.

I quickly slipped the folder out of the file cabinet and into my great, massive brown leather East German *Grundschule* book satchel. It was a matter of instants before I was out the door and down the stairs, and out the front door, and into my charming lavender Volkswagen Beetle automobile.

That evening, in my fireplace, the Edward T. LeJeune file burned very, very nicely.

CHAPTER 11

Dear Willie Mays,

It's fun to be a writer. Here's something I wrote that I like.

I'm thinking of a nice place to be. The nicest place. In my bed with my dog Godzilla. Taking a nap while she watches over me. If monsters come, she will chase them away and I can sleep all I want. Naps are good. Not when someone wakes you up though. Godzilla would never let anyone wake me up from my nap.

Richard wants a dog but his parents'll never give him one. If he had one, he could bring him over to play with Godzilla. It's good to have a good friend to share things with.

thank you for listening.

your pal,

Toby

P.S.
How wunderbar (!!!!) to have a private diary that's actually private! Ha ha ha!

It was with great relish that, one bright and sunny afternoon, while the children were out at recess, running, running, sweating, sweating, throwing up, throwing up, I put down my knitting and raised my elegant, strong body from behind my gleaming teacher's desk and cruised between the students' tidy little desks to the messy desk of young Tobias Wilcox.

I had not read his personal, private journal in several days and was yearning to see what his little fertile mind had been up to.

Squashing the desire to put on chemical-resistant hazmat gloves, I raised the lid of his desk and rummaged through the usual damp, disgusting mess. And rummaged. And rummaged. I had great hope, but unfortunately his personal, private journal was not there.

Was this a problem for Mrs. Ravenbach? No, it was not!

If you are well prepared, nothing is a problem. And Mrs.

Ravenbach was well prepared, as you will recall, since she was in possession of her own personal mole. A bald-headed one named Richard.

Through the window, I quickly got his attention and summoned him to my lovely classroom that smelled so delightfully of Pine-Sol.

It only took a small amount of Adam's apple pinching to get Richard to go to the playground, to slide young Tobias Wilcox's dirty journal from his backpack, and to lay it on the well-polished surface of my teacher's desk.

I noticed that the journal was more dusty than usual. A strange silver dust, but no matter.

I let Richard stand there, at a discreet distance, of course, and watch me learn of his friend's innermost thoughts. The guilt and shame Richard felt would go a long way toward preventing in the future his using mud puddle language. While he fidgeted, I found out precisely what Tobias's devious little mind had been up to.

The answer, once I was able to decipher his atrocious handwriting, was that his fertile little mind had been up to ... *wonderful things*! Thoughts and musings about the life, the teaching, and the overall relationship between the child and his teacher. It was quite gratifying to behold.

I'm so happy that Mrs. Ravenbach is my teacher cause she taught me many amazing things. Plant structures and functions. The solar system, the Golden Rule, the twelve times table, possessive pronouns, the importance of physical fitness (and not just for playing!), about symphony music, Beethoven especially. He is now my favorite musician. I like him even more than I like the Beatles.

After my parent teacher conference, I decided to rededicate myself to learning. To follow the path down which Mrs. Ravenbach is leading me.

She's the cleverest teacher I ever had. It's a great idea to do whatever she tells me to do! Learning is so much fun! I loooooove fourth grade!

And I'm so excited about my poem!
I want to write a poem about Papi,
my grandfather!
About how I love climbing up high
high high at the top of his tobacco
barn and how the sunlight comes
down through the air and you can
see the sun in the air. Plus, the
tobacco barn smells _awesome_.
Specially if you like to smoke
cigars. Papi liked great, big, giant,
fat ones. Someday I'd like to
smoke a big, giant, fat cigar
so I can be like my wonderful
grandfather!

THE AUTHENTIC AND VENERABLE CAMARADERIE OF SUBMARINE ENTHUSIASTS

The April 20th McKegway School Sub Club meeting was called to order by President Wilcox. Recording Secretary Kaliski kept the minutes. Minutes from the last meeting were approved by unanimous vote of the entire Sub Club membership.

Vigorous discussion of whether to put butter on the jelly side of peanut butter and jelly sandwiches for the upcoming Sub Club regatta at Lake Ruppenthal. Sergeant-at-Arms Arthur Hester suggested we try both ways after school on Thursday and decide. Agreed and approved.

Short discussion of whether to drink Dr. Pepper or lemonade at regatta. Decision made to buy both varieties of refreshment.

Short discussion between President Wilcox and ergeant-at-Arms Hester of upcoming Poetry Contest. Discussion tabled by Secretary Kaliski as irrelevant to the Sub Club mission statement. If we had one.

Lengthy and spirited discussion of whether Secretary Kaliski could borrow his father's walkie-talkies for the Lake Ruppenthal regatta. Secretary Kaliski was in the "Anti" column. President Wilcox was in the "Pro" column. Decision made that Secretary Kaliski should ask Mr. Kaliski, and, should Mr. Kaliski refuse permission to borrow said walkie-talkies, to borrow them anyway. Resolved to take photographs of walkie-talkies on the shelf before said borrowing, so as to return them to exactly precisely the correct location. It is reflected in the minutes that sometimes Mr. Kaliski is a jerk.

Lively discussion of whether Alka-Seltzer plugs would be preferable to sugar cubes in steel shot ballast tank discharge tubes. Resolved to proceed with Alka-Seltzer.

Brief, tense, near violent discussion of whether to admit girls in the Sub Club. Sergeant-at-Arms Hester was loudly in opposition to President Wilcox's desire to make this change in the Bylaws. Secretary Kaliski was undecided. There was some yelling.

Meeting suddenly adjourned when Mrs. Wilcox arrived with brownies and milk and Cheetos.

Yum yum.

Signed: Toby Wilcox, president. Richard Kaliski, Secretary. Arthur Hester, sergeant-at-arms.

It was so gratifying to be seeing my knowledge so well received by my young pupil!

Miracles do happen. And young Tobias Wilcox might be my miracle child for this school year.

I closed his diary. It held no more interest for me.

Suffice to say, the important thing was that young Tobias Wilcox was *back on track*! Good job by the teacher!

It was a bright and sunny day when Mrs. Hamilton's fourth grade class filed into my classroom for the fourth grade portion of the All-School Poetry Contest. They were silent, respectful, and had their heads bowed. It was clear, because her head too was bowed, that Mrs. Hamilton was terrified of me.

The terror. Always the correct idea.

One by one, each little child shuffled to the front of my tidy classroom and, knees knocking, upper lips perspiring, and fingers twisting nervously as their hands clasped and unclasped behind their backs, each child said the stupid little poem that they had composed.

One by one, each of the little children disgraced himself or herself.

Trevania Sumner had a boring poem about a teapot. It had a wretched rhyme scheme.

Arthur Hester said a poem about James Bond, but it made absolutely no sense to anyone on the planet except Arthur Hester himself.

Ernie Harbison said a poem about how he wanted to grow up and be a Marine. What a ridiculous subject for a poem.

Drusilla Tanner, to my dismay, recited a poem . . . about the

My Papi

I miss my grandfather.
We used to go riding on his farm.
He had a battered blue rusted pickup truck.
I would ride on the tailgate.
Papi was busy. Always working. He had
strong, strong hands.
And a smile. Always a smile for me.
If I fell off the tailgate, he would wait
for me to catch up.
He told me I was his best friend.
I remember the smells of his cigar.
The enormous tobacco barn.
Sun shining through the slat walls.
That warm summer tobacco smell.
He had rough hands. But gentle when he
held mine.
I loved my Papi.
I loved to look at his hands.
They were so old. Scars and thick veins
and wrinkles.
But strong and talented.
His dog was Rex. Rex and Papi were
never apart.
Both of them were old, old, old.
Rex would sleep.
At Papi's feet. And Papi would read
the comic strips to me.
When I was little.
But he would get tired. Because he was
old. Sleepy.
And he would nod his head. Nodding.
Nodding. And finally stop reading.
And so, that gentle man and dog, they
slept together.

farting. Her poem was quite popular with the boys, especially Arthur and Richard and their fat little friend Tobias Wilcox. Needless to say, she did not get chosen.

I mention Tobias Wilcox only at the end of my discussion of the poetry recital for a very marvelous reason.

Much to my surprise, and it is rare that Mrs. Ravenbach finds herself surprised, young Tobias Wilcox had crafted a most excellent poem. *Wunderbar.* Not only did he say it beautifully, but it was a *superb* piece of writing. I was astounded anyone so headstrong could write something so beautiful.

The entire poem from the beginning to the middle to the end, was *wunderbar.*

It reminded me of my own long-dead, much-beloved *Grossvater.* Everyone should be so lucky to have a grandfather like mine, and so few do. When Tobias had finished reciting his poem, with that touching final line, there were several girls dabbing their eyes from the tears.

"Tobias, that was excellent."

"Thank you, Mrs. Ravenbach. I spent a long time writing it, and an even longer time rewriting it. The stuff you told us about how you're supposed to rewrite stuff was real helpful."

"It was an excellent poem. Mrs. Hamilton and I will now decide who will get to represent the fourth grade in the All-School Poetry Contest."

It did not take long for Mrs. Hamilton and myself to decide that young Tobias Wilcox should be the one to represent the fourth grade with his most excellent poem about his *Grossvater.* Especially since Mrs. Hamilton said not a word. When we told the class young Tobias was indeed the winner, they exploded with the kind of applause normally reserved for a ship launching. It was heart-warming. He was smiling and happy and overflowing with the self-confidence. It was a wonderful educational moment. The only thing that tainted the moment for me was the fact that young Tobias Wilcox was grinning, as the Southerners say, "like a mule eating briars," because he seemed *so* certain he would be chosen to represent the fourth grade in the All-School Poetry Contest.

His grinning made me want to smack him in the face. I restrained myself. Barely.

Despite my nearly overpowering desire to leave my hand-print on his cheek, I was proud of young Tobias Wilcox. He had done the best job. Mrs. Hamilton, *natürlich*, agreed with me.

After Mrs. Hamilton's class left, I said, "Tobias?"

"Yes, Mrs. Ravenbach?"

"You deserve a special, special reward for winning the fourth grade portion of the All-School Poetry Contest."

"Really, Mrs. Ravenbach?"

"Would you like to brush my hair or massage my feet?"

Every child froze in place.

Young Tobias Wilcox had never been invited to enjoy the Highest Honor. He had never participated in Reward Time.

He said, "Thank you and no thank you."

I could not have been more astounded if a polar bear ran in and shouted, "The Father Christmas is a Communist agitator!" Never, in all my years of teaching, had I heard a pupil refuse the Highest Honor. This confirmed my suspicion that, when he was a small child, young Tobias must have been dropped on his head by his parents.

"Everyone wants to brush my hair. Everyone wants to rub

my tired feet, especially when I allow them to use my fragrant unguent from Westfalen."

"I don't know what unguent is," he said, "but I don't want to touch your feet. I bet they smell."

The room became extraordinarily quiet.

"Excuse me?"

His eyes, like a little snake, they did not blink. He just looked up at me, and looked up at me, and looked up at me.

He was a most vexing child.

"Are you certain you are not wishing to rub my feet or brush my hair? I will let you use my sterling silver hairbrushes and comb." He shook his little head.

Arthur said, "Toby, it's the best thing you can imagine. We all love to brush Mrs. Ravenbach's hair."

Drusilla said, "And everybody likes to massage her feet! The lotion smells so wonderful on your hands for the rest of the day."

And . . . then . . .

Young Tobias Wilcox said . . . "Oh, barf."

At that precise instant, something dreadful occurred.

Every child in the classroom began to *laugh*.

And laugh, and laugh, and laugh!

They had obviously been holding back their laughter for quite some many months now. It *exploded* like the *Hindenburg*. Not a quiet, peaceful little laugh either; it was a gigantic, mirthful, percussive, loud, and awful laugh. It was the most embarrassing laugh I have ever heard in my entire lifetime. And it was directed at *me*, Mrs. Leni Ravenbach, fourth grade teacher. Whatever happened to Mother. Father. Teacher. God?

As they howled, their mouths were open so wide, I could

see all the way down to their tonsils. Tears were squirting out of their eyes and running down their cheeks. Drusilla was pounding her desk with her skinny little fist so hard that her scruffy nail polish flaked off and landed on the desk. Richard was bobbing his bald head up and down so fast, it looked blurry. Even Larry, the little suckup, was laughing. Arthur Hester, who never said anything, who never did anything, never thought anything, never felt anything . . . was laughing at *me*, Mrs. Ravenbach, his teacher!

They were all laughing *at me*!

Tobias Wilcox stood there, smiling and smiling and smiling and *smiling* and smiling.

CHAPTER 12

The sun had set, darkness had set in, and I was setting, ha-ha, the table for tea when I heard a light little knock at my door. Mrs. Button! My dear friend.

She was wearing a lovely little print dress, her nicest feathered hat, and white kid gloves. I do adore a woman who wears gloves. A sign of the good breeding. So few Americans had the good breeding. I was honored to know one, at least.

I opened the door. She came across the room, light as air, on beautiful white high-heeled shoes. The heels made such a pleasing sound on my hardwood floor. I do adore a woman who sees the point of dressing up for the tea. These Americans, they are so sloppy about everything. Dungarees, tracksuits, sweatpants! It's astounding they could put a man on the moon!

Mrs. Button sat down across from me and crossed her legs at the ankles. She was shivering with the worry, the fear, and the vexation.

"Mrs. Button," I said, "it seems you have a story to share."

She frowned. "Late this afternoon, I was over at the Wilcoxes' home."

"Do tell." Because I was serving the tea, I pretended I was English.

"Mrs. Wilcox, because she is much younger, relies on me for advice on how to raise her son. We are confidantes. I come and go in their house quite freely. On this occasion, I let myself in the front door and gave a small, 'Anybody home . . . ?' I approached their kitchen. There was quite a commotion. Toby had come home from school with stories of your classroom today."

I leaned forward.

"He was telling how you had asked him if he wanted to brush your hair or massage your feet . . . I thought, my precious Leni, you had resolved never to grant him the Highest Honor."

"The child wrote an excellent poem. He will be representing the grade in the All-School Poetry Contest. No student from my class has ever *won* the Poetry Contest . . . I felt he deserved the reward. Perhaps I miscalculated."

"Apparently he turned down the Highest Honor."

"To my surprise and consternation, yes."

"The Wilcox family, including the dog, was quite amused by the tale he recounted."

"Surely I did not hear you say 'amused'?"

Her voice, her face, and every molecule of her being were as hard as Krupp steel. "When I tiptoed in, they were . . . *laughing*."

My fingers froze on my exquisite Meissen teacup.

She said, "Do you not think it is time you took . . . executive action?"

Then my exquisite Meissen teacup shattered.

It did not take long for me to finish tea with my dear friend, Mrs. Button. It did not take long for me to usher her out the door. It did not take long for me to clean up the sadly broken cup, to clear away the teapot, cozy, tray, lemon slices, and clean the *Apfelstrudel* crumbs from my W. Schillig silk sofa. It did not take long for me to pour myself a generous tumbler of *Schnaps*. Nor did it take long for me to drink it. Or the next one. Or the next one. None of *that* took long.

What did take a long, long time was for my great, big, strong wonderful heart to slow its racing pace.

A superb teacher must, from time to time, face difficult situations. The teaching is very, very important work, and, as the fourth grade is the most important year in all of the education, so the demands upon the fourth grade teacher are stringent, rigorous, and, occasionally, heart-wrenching.

When one is at the top of one's field, and one is called upon to make difficult, difficult decisions, one must rise to the occasion. Like cream, rising sweetly to the top.

And that is what I did.

I am remembering particularly well that particular day.

I was in a particularly pleasant mood. Things had gone well with the mathematics instruction. Things had gone well with the reading after lunch. Things had gone well with the recess. Drusilla Tanner had made a particularly marvelous oral report on *From the Mixed-Up Files of Mrs. Basil E. Frankweiler.*

"Drusilla?"

"Yes, ma'am?"

Dear Willie,

Me. Safe. Happy.

"Would you like to brush my hair?"

"Oh, yes, ma'am."

"Your report was very well constructed and I think I should reward you."

"Can I go get the comb and mirror and hairbrushes?"

"May I."

"*May* I go get the comb and mirror and hairbrushes, Mrs. Ravenbach? Please?"

I so enjoyed when the children were eager for their Reward. It makes things so much more pleasurable for me and for the children and for the classroom and for the learning and, *natürlich,* for the order and the discipline.

"Drusilla?"

"Yes, ma'am?"

"Do you know where I keep my sterling silver hairbrushes and mirror and comb?"

She nodded so hard I thought her pigtails would snap off.

"Would you please go and get them?"

The beautiful child fairly skipped to the red velvet pillow where I keep my great-great-grandmother's silver sterling hairbrushes, mirror, and comb.

As I began to take down my long, heavy, blond braids, I smiled inwardly at the thought of having my hair brushed. I do love it so. Then I heard a small voice from the far, far end of the classroom. Drusilla's small voice. Drusilla's small, tiny, wee . . . *frightened* voice.

"Mrs. Ravenbach . . . ?"

"What, child?"

"They aren't . . . *here.*"

"Are you certain?"

"Yes, Mrs. Ravenbach. I've searched very carefully."

"As carefully as the little chicken when she is searching for the last little piece of grain?"

"Of course, Mrs. Ravenbach. That's how you taught us to find things."

"Well then, please, my dear, look again to make sure. This is quite serious."

All my pupils were sitting straight up at their desks, backs rigid, little eyes focused on the blackboard. The order and the discipline, the basis for everything in the civilization. All the students heard much rummaging.

"Mrs. Ravenbach, they're not here!"

"Drusilla . . ."

"They really aren't here!"

Every single student in the entire classroom sucked in their breath. It sounded as if an elephant had sat on a basketball.

At that precise moment, what was young Tobias Wilcox doing? Picking his nose.

I got up from my elegant teacher's desk and ran across the classroom. In the history of my teaching career, I had never run. Running is undignified and I don't believe students should see a teacher exerting herself in any other way than the teaching.

Instantly I was at the back of the classroom. Instantly, in the gold-trimmed red velvet pillow, I saw the indentation left by my sterling silver hairbrushes, mirror, and comb. My *missing* sterling silver hairbrushes, mirror, and comb!

My voice was terrible to behold. "Someone has *stolen* my sterling silver hairbrushes, mirror, and comb. They were given to me by my great-great-grandmother. They are made from the finest silver from the Harz Mountains, the region in Germany that produces the most exquisite work."

I tried to calm my breathing. I failed.

"Who has stolen my sterling silver hairbrushes, mirror, and comb?!"

The class was as still as a dead, dry mouse in a dark basement corner.

"Drusilla?"

"Yes, Mrs. Ravenbach."

"Do you have any idea who might have stolen the sterling silver hairbrushes, mirror, and comb belonging to your beloved teacher?"

She shook her head. Her tightly braided pigtails flew around.

"Does *anyone* have any idea who might have stolen their beloved teacher's sterling silver hairbrushes, mirror, and comb?"

Not one child breathed.

Not one child passed the gas. That was rare.

A good teacher does not show her anger, ever. A good teacher has a death camp look. I have an *excellent* death camp look. I gave them mine. At no charge! Ha-ha. A joke.

"I have no idea where it is."

"Beats me."

"I dunno."

"Mrs. Ravenbach, I don't know. I swear."

"Maybe they're under the pillow?"

"Can I . . . go to the bathroom?" This from Arthur Hester. He was always wanting to go to the bathroom. What he needed was a good smack on the behind with a riding crop.

"Everyone, *stand up!*" I said.

All together, all at once, the sound was satisfying: *smack,* their little bottoms unstuck themselves from their wooden chairs. *Smack,* their little feet hit the ground. *Smack,* their little heels clacked together like a formation of Prussian cavalry officers.

I cast my eyes on every single student. One by one. All were looking straight ahead at the blackboard. Well, almost all . . .

Little Tobias Wilcox was watching me.

My voice, I must confess, had a bit of an *edge.*

"I want every child in this fourth grade classroom to open his or her desk, to slide his hands in his desk or her hands in her desk, and remove every single item from inside that desk and lay them on the floor beside that desk. Right now. Go."

There came two dozen scurrying noises like two dozen scurrying cats escaping from a twelve-foot-tall Doberman pinscher as my beloved students rummaged in their desks and pulled sticky gum and comic books and school books and notebooks and pencils and more gum and hairbrushes, but not mine, and lunch sacks and pencils and pencils, some which were nearly chewed into pieces.

I supervised the unloading process. My hairbrushes did not appear. Each child was staring straight at the blackboard as a good and teachable fourth grade student ought. Except for Tobias Wilcox.

Little Tobias Wilcox was watching me.

As I marched straight to the desk of young Tobias Wilcox,

my elegant high heels made a satisfying sound on my soft Bokhara rug.

On the floor beside his desk, he had a pile of debris so high that the cow that jumped over the moon couldn't jump over it. A few school books, of course, incredibly messy with holes poked in them and mustaches drawn on patriots' faces . . . quite disrespectful. A bird's nest, a Lego man, DunkAroos, peppermints with no wrappers, a baseball glove and ball, three fishing lures, a magnifying glass, three sets of car keys from God knows what automobiles, baseball cards and more baseball cards, and trash, trash, trash, but not my sterling silver hairbrushes, mirror, and comb.

I did see his hands in his lap, trembling. His knee was tapping. His little chin was quivering. I must say I could see the words "I'm about to tell a lie" written in beautiful cursive right across his lumpy little face.

"Young Wilcox," I said with my almost sternest voice. He was shivering. "Young Wilcox, have you removed every single thing from your desk?"

He said, slowly, "Yes, ma'am."

He was telling a black lie. "Are you certain?"

"Yes . . . ma'am."

"Are you positively one hundred percent absolutely certain?"

"Yes, ma'am."

"Because the most important thing in the classroom is you know what?"

"The telling . . . of the truth."

"Yes, isn't it? So I'm going to ask you one more time: have you removed everything from the interior of your desk?"

"Yes, ma'am." His little voice was so small, all the students were leaning forward to be able to hear him lie, the little lying wretch. I must say he was not a very good liar; I have seen better. But, little fellow, he was trying his hardest.

I enjoyed that I was able to make his fat little chin quiver. Why? Because it meant I had gotten his attention.

"Tobias."

"Yes, Mrs. Ravenbach?"

"Open your desk." He did nothing. "Open your *desk*." My voice was as dark and bitter as week-old coffee grounds soaked in vinegar. "Look at me, you miserable little boy." Everyone gasped.

He shook his head. I could tell his heart was not in it, pathetic child. He was like a prisoner being led to the gallows. He did not want to take a step, but he knew that he must. He also knew what the end result was going to be.

"Open your desk, young Tobias."

"No, ma'am."

"Step away from the desk. Right this instant." He did nothing. I called out to Sophie Taschlin. "Miss Taschlin?"

"Yes, Mrs. Ravenbach?"

"Come here, please."

"Yes, Mrs. Ravenbach."

She was there in a flash. I've always liked her. Such an obedient and beautiful child.

"Mr. Wilcox, scoot back from your desk seven and a half inches, please." Using the students' last names when they're about to be in trouble makes the situation so much more memorable for them, don't you think? Young Wilcox scooted back fourteen inches, but I decided not to bring out the tape measure this time.

"Sophie?"

"Yes, Mrs. Ravenbach."

"Please search the interior of Mr. Wilcox's desk and remove anything in it that you might find."

I shall remember for many, many, years the heartless "I've got you in my sights, you worm" look that dear, sweet Sophie Taschlin gave young Tobias Wilcox. Miss Taschlin stuck her angelic hand inside Tobias's nasty desk.

She was such a pretty child with the longest blond hair. Perhaps when I die I will leave to her in my will my sterling silver hairbrushes, mirror, and comb. I saw the triumph and glee on her little face as she closed her hand around an object and slowly withdrew from Tobias Wilcox's desk . . . one of my sterling silver hairbrushes! Followed instantly by its mate, mirror, and comb!

In all my twenty-one years of teaching I had never found reason to raise my voice with a student.

"TOBIAS WILCOX!!" If I practiced a bit more I might be able to shatter a wineglass were it a fine enough glass. Young Wilcox was stiff, like a week-old corpse. "WHAT ARE THOSE?!"

He looked at me with the fiery flame of hatred in his eyes. *Natürlich.*

"Miss Taschlin?"

"Yes, Mrs. Ravenbach?"

"What have you got in your hands? Please share with the other students."

"Your silver sterling hairbrushes, mirror, and comb, Mrs. Ravenbach."

"YOU, TOBIAS WILCOX, ARE NOTHING MORE THAN A COMMON *THIEF!*"

He shrank back. In shock. In fear. His eyes became wet. He shook like a sail flapping in a hurricane. It was delightfully satisfying. I had reached the child! I *had his attention!*

I switched my voice to my softest inside-quiet-mouse voice. All the students leaned even more forward. "Young Wilcox? *Why* have you stolen my silver hairbrushes, mirror, and comb?"

His voice was tiny. "I didn't." I looked at him. He looked at me. For the longest time neither of us blinked.

I said, "I am going to give you one more chance to come clean, as they say in the detective shows, young Wilcox. Why. Did. You. Steal. My sterling silver hairbrushes and mirror and comb?"

He was so close to crying in front of all of the other students, I thought for a moment he would burst into tears and drown us all, but he held back the flood and mumbled, "I . . . did . . . not . . ."

"You have been caught red-handed. Every student in the classroom sees my sterling silver hairbrushes and mirror and comb on your desk. Every student knows that you are not telling the truth, and in a classroom the truth telling is the most important thing, is it not?" He was shaking so hard, he could barely nod.

From the back came a gasp. I am not completely positive, but it sounded like Lisbet Quinteros. Her horrified gasp was picked up and went around like electricity. There was a loud inhaling as if all the air had left the room at once.

I looked down at young Mr. Wilcox. On the floor beneath his chair was a puddle of light yellow pee-pee.

I smiled triumphantly and said, "Is there anyone here who needs to use the toilet?"

No one raised their hand.

"Is there anyone *here* who needs to use the toilet?"

There was the longest pause and the little boy, one slow pathetic time, nodded.

"Then I suppose you should get up and leave the class in the middle of our session and take care of your problem, young Tobias Wilcox, and when you come back we shall discuss the theft of my sterling silver hairbrushes, mirror, and comb. Is that clear?"

He only managed a pathetic nod, which is no surprise because he was a pathetic child. He got up, dripping on the floor, and walked shamefacedly with his head bowed down, no doubt under the weight of his crime and the embarrassment of having peed in his little pants in front of all of his little chums.

I said in my most clear voice, "Normally, a child who steals would be sent to the principal's office for swift justice and painful retribution. But, I am thinking we have all learned a marvelous lesson here in the classroom today. So. That is that!" I clapped my hands and smiled brightly.

All of young Tobias's chums were not so very chummy as they laughed and laughed and laughed when he walked in front of the desks, in front of the blackboard, in front of my beautiful globe of the world, toward the doorway. I could tell by the way he was walking that, with each step, the doorway was getting further and further away, as if he was living in a nightmare . . . a nightmare that, *natürlich,* was his own doing.

While he was gone I sat down and made notes for the parent-teacher conference I knew was sure to come.

Dear Willie,

It's awful to be a kid. To be afraid. To wanna say something and not be able to make your mouth work or any sounds to come outta your guts.
Somehow it's worse than anything.

What I am is many things. Some are fantastic. Like yakkin with my dad when we play catch or helping my mom pick up the oranges when she spilled them in the grocery store. Some are not fantastic. One time, I ate a booger. Another time, I flushed a firecracker down a commode.

What I am not, is a thief and a liar. Ever.

thanks for listening,
 your pal,
 Toby

CHAPTER 13

Unlike the painful parent-teacher conferences of some teachers at the McKegway School for Clever and Gifted Children, *my* parent-teacher conferences are always successful. I enjoy welcoming the parents into my classroom. They can visit their child's cubby. They can see the child's desk. On the wall, they can see the colorful pictures the child has made, all evidence of a wonderful time spent in Mrs. Ravenbach's wonderful fourth grade classroom.

When Mr. and Mrs. Wilcox and young Tobias came into my classroom, I was knitting at my desk, in front of which I had placed three small chairs. The only grown-up chair in the room being mine, of course. I imagine they felt a tiny bit uncomfortable on those little chairs.

When the Wilcox family was settled down for the year's final parent-teacher conference, I gently laid down my knitting, cracked my knuckles, and looked straight into the eyes of young Tobias.

It was oh-so-clear that he was wanting to murder me.

I could see it in his tightly clenched fat little fists. His fat little body was consumed by anger. Consumed by anger is not a way to go into a difficult conversation that one has any desire to win.

He knew that I had been reading his journal. Otherwise, why would he have written all that claptrap about what a wonderful teacher I was? Just because the teachers tell children we do not read their personal, private journals does not mean we do not read them! Only a *child* would be so naive to think that their teacher would not be reading their journal, if knowing what was in that journal might be helpful to the teacher in the orderly running of the classroom.

Of course, ha-ha, they *are* children, aren't they?

"Good afternoon, Mr. and Mrs. Wilcox." I was smiling my finest white-teeth smile. It is very difficult to withstand the force of such a wonderful smile, from such a wonderful teacher. Yet, incredibly, Mr. Wilcox resisted.

"I want to know what's going on here."

"Please, Mr. Wilcox, you tell me."

"Toby said you stuck the hairbrushes the children use to brush your hair with in his desk, and you said he stole them from you."

"That is what he said?"

"Yes." The fat little boy was nodding his head vigorously.

I said, "That is not what happened."

Mr. Wilcox's voice had an angry, irritated tone. "Now listen here, Mrs. Ravenbach! We didn't—" Instantly, Mrs. Wilcox gave Mr. Wilcox a *look.* Wives are always full of the *looks.* Oh, my, my, my, my. After *that* particular species of look, Mr. Wilcox wasn't going to say too much more. I gave him the full force of my charm and gentility, along with a most pleasing smile.

Mrs. Wilcox spoke next "Toby's not happy. He's not doing well, and we're concerned."

"You should be. He is a thief. I would be most concerned if my child were a thief."

"Toby told us he didn't take your hairbrushes."

"And comb."

"Yes, Mrs. Ravenbach, and comb. Toby didn't take them."

"And mirror. Every child saw them. In his desk. There is no way he did not take them, despite what he may have said to you at the home, far, far from the classroom.

"He told us he had no idea how they got in his desk. That somebody else must've put them there."

"Absolute poppycock."

I must say, the look young Tobias gave me at our *last* parent-teacher conference, the one that would split me into sixteen pieces had he actually had laser beams in his eyes, that look was *nothing* compared to the look which he next gave me. I began to feel the heat growing up the back of my neck and under my bottom on my chair. I decided I wanted to end this parent-teacher conference quickly and on a pleasant note. So I did.

"Mr. and Mrs. Wilcox, are you aware that a student *saw* Tobias take my sterling silver hairbrushes, mirror, and comb from their place on the red velvet pillow in the back of the classroom and hide them in his desk?"

Mr. Wilcox gurgled like he was going to drown right here in the middle of my classroom. How unattractive.

I said, "Did Tobias not inform you of this?"

Mrs. Wilcox said, "No . . ."

"I am not surprised. Mrs. Wilcox, I am so, so, so sorry. Sometimes children enjoy telling the lies."

"Not Toby. He never lies about anything. He's the most truthful child I've ever known."

"Well, in this case that is not the case."

Mr. Wilcox said, "Who's the kid who ratted him out?"

"I am afraid I am not at liberty to divulge confidential information, but suffice to say, a student came to me when I was alone in my classroom and said she had information that I should hear. She repeated that information to Principal Hertenstein and it is abundantly clear that your child, Mr. and Mrs. Wilcox, is a thief."

Mr. Wilcox said, "But he told us he didn't do it and I believe him. That's the kind of kid he is. He always tells the truth."

"Mr. Wilcox, I have been teaching the fourth grade for twenty-nine years and one thing I am knowing about children is that sometimes they are telling the lies."

Mr. and Mrs. Wilcox, they nodded. They knew.

The expression on that little boy's face, I must confess to you, it was magnificent. Watching the sad realization dawn on him that he was being defeated by me, his teacher, made every effort on my part worthwhile. I saw the fear. A wonderful emotion to see in a pupil. Because, without the fear, you cannot then have the respect. Through the respect is a teacher able to maintain in the classroom the order and the discipline.

And, after the fear, of course, the terror.

I was simply trying to help the young student, and his family, with the mess they had made of their lives.

Or the mess they were going to make of their lives.

Without me.

And my wonderful influence.

Mrs. Wilcox said, "Why would he lie?"

I then spoke the two sentences that I had been up all night writing. They had come to me a little after three o'clock in the morning, and after several generous snifters of cherry *Schnaps*. I smiled pleasantly and said, "I am a teacher. Why would I lie?"

The pure beauty of my eight well-crafted words took all three members of the Wilcox family by surprise.

Why would the teacher lie? She has nothing to gain, nothing at stake. There is nothing in it for the teacher, no reason, no explanation for why the teacher would lie.

The child has every reason to lie. He is a child, after all. Most things they get, they get by telling the lies. Big lies, little lies. Black lies, white lies, fibs. It is what they know.

They do it all the time, the little animals.

"Perhaps young Tobias stole the sterling silver hairbrushes and mirror and comb that my great-great-grandmother had given me because he wanted to sell them on the black market. Or perhaps he wanted to cause me emotional pain or embarrassment. Or perhaps for some other, unknown reason. In any event, he took them. They were found in his desk. He wanted them. He took them. Everyone in the classroom saw them in his desk. Everyone in the classroom is knowing that your son is a thief."

Tobias said nothing. He was having a little bit of trouble with his breathing.

"So, Principal Hertenstein and I have decided for young

Tobias's future development that it is imperative he *repeat the fourth grade.*"

There followed a long period of quiet, quiet silence.

Mrs. Wilcox said, "Toby, do you have anything to say?"

Naturally, the child had nothing to say. Other than a barely audible, "No. No, ma'am."

Naturally, *I* had something to say.

I said, "Mrs. Wilcox. Principal Hertenstein, as he has a low regard for thieves, came very, very close to expelling Tobias from the McKegway School for Clever and Gifted Children. It required every ounce of my eloquence to convince him not to. Your son Tobias is very lucky he is not at this very moment slumped in a sloppy gutter filled with gum wrappers and wet cigar butts, but instead has the great good fortune to be coming to a wonderful school next year and enjoying the fourth grade. Again." I looked at young Tobias Wilcox. "You are the luckiest little boy in this entire city."

"Expelled?" said his mother, her voice about to break from the tears that I could see on the edges of her eyes. She had beautiful blue eyes. I wondered why young Tobias had such ugly pig-like eyes, when his mother had such gorgeous ones.

My voice was as hard as San Francisco Bay when a person lands on it after jumping from the Golden Gate Bridge. "I would advise you to count your blessings. Repeating the fourth grade is not that awful. Going to the penitentiary later in life because one was expelled from the finest school in the city is very, very awful."

His parents did not hear young Tobias softly whisper, "Someday, something horrible is going to happen to you . . ."

When I said, "I doubt that," I gave a small cough, for camou-
flage. The little boy's parents, again, did not hear. I am a master at
the cough-talking.

Because they were so upset, this family needed the beauty of
my smile shining down upon them. I could see that it gave com-
fort to Mr. and Mrs. Wilcox as they lifted their fat little boy and
dragged him from my classroom.

Truly, the most satisfying moment of my teaching career!

I sat at my desk with my back erect, feet flat on the floor, my
big, hard belly and grand bosom jutting out proudly. I picked up
my knitting and patted my big, hard belly. I rubbed it. I patted it
again. You don't get a solid belly like this without excellent breeding and a *lot* of *Strudel*. The sun came shining in my beautiful
classroom. All was right with the world. I had taught a child a
valuable lesson. He would go through life, having repeated the
fourth grade, secure in the knowledge that his teacher loved him
and cared for him even more, perhaps, than his own parents.

I heard the Wilcox family whispering in the hallway.

In an instant, on my toes, I was across the room. My elegant
Christian Louboutin high heels made no sound on my Bokhara
rug as I slipped delicately as a ballet dancer to the open doorway.

The tone of voice Mr. Wilcox was using pleased me no end,
the totally correct tone of voice to use with a child who was about
to repeat the fourth grade. He said, sounding quite a bit like
Darth Vader, "Do you have any idea how much this is going to
cost?"

Mrs. Wilcox said, "We could take in boarders. My mother has
alway—"

"Not a snowball's chance. Don't ever forget, your dad was *happy* when he got cancer."

I distinctly and clearly heard Mrs. Wilcox say, "Toby, Toby, Toby! Why on earth did you steal your teacher's hairbrushes?" Nothing could be more thrilling for a teacher than to know she has driven a wedge between parent and child! For the parent to mistrust the child in comparison to the teacher is an amazing and wonderful thing.

"I didn't . . . steal her stupid . . . stuff. She put it in my desk so . . . you won't . . . believe me . . . She's horrible . . . and you're *worse*, you . . . don't . . . believe me either."

Music to my ears. Like the *click, click, click* of my antique ivory knitting needles.

Between the teacher and the student, everyone will always believe the teacher.

Because it is the teacher who is always, always telling the truth.

This's what I wanted to say to her so, so, so bad—

"You just wanna win Teacher of the Year! That's all you want, other than see how mean you can be! You're the meanest teacher in the world! You're the meanest teacher in the history of teaching! I bet Hitler's teacher wasn't as mean as you! You're a dirty liar! I can't believe you won four Golden Apples! I can't believe they let you teach rock collecting, much less something as important as fourth grade! I can't believe you're acting this way, you're disgusting! I've never heard of anyone as mean as you! I'll get even with you if it's the last thing I ever do!"

Did I say that?
NO.
Stupid idiot moron stupidface wimp.

Dear Willie,

You know how much it hurts to have something to say and be too afraid to say it? I bet that's never happened to you. It's happened to me. Specially lately.

I didn't used to be this way. I swear. I used to be okay.

"Who Dares, Wins," right? I can't stay like this. I'll rot. Or worse. Who Dares, Wins!

I'm going to get her.
I'm going to get her.
I'm going to get her.
I'm going to get her.
I'm going to get her.

I'm going to get her. I'm going to get her. I'm going to get her. I'm going to get her!!!

Okay. Calm down. Breathe. Make a plan. Plans're good. Think.

Think.

"This's Zip Tuggle and it's a beautiful day here at Giants Stadium. It's the bottom of the ninth. Tie game. Bases loaded. Two outs. Wilcox steps up to the plate, kicking dirt from his cleats... Ace reporters from the Mckegway *Gazette* are scribbling down Wilcox's every move."

Think.

"As forty two thousand five hundred and twelve screaming fans go wild, Wilcox faces Koufax with steely-eyed determination."

Think.

"Here's the wind up. The throw. A heater! AND WILCOX <u>BUNTS</u>! A PERFECT BUNT! OH MY GOLLY! He takes off for first base like a scalded dog. Campanella dives for the ball, bobbles it! DROPS IT while Wilcox rounds first, screaming for second base!"

<u>Plan #1</u>
Bad plan... at least it's a plan.

"Derek Jeter scrambles from short, rifles it to Jackie Robinson, who's ready to make the tag, but Wilcox head fakes him and blows past, on toward third base! OH MY GOLLY! He's SLIIIIIDING! Like a comet blazing straight at Brooks Robinson! And the throw from Jackie to Brooks! Wilcox is never gonna make it!"

Plan #2

Bad plan... worse, actually.

What I need's a Co-Conspirator. With red lipstick and a nickel-plated .38. But she'd need a trench coat and a slouch hat. Does Drusie's mom have a slouch hat? Mine sure doesn't.

Plan #3

Bad plan...

"IN A CLOUD OF GIANTS STADIUM DUST, HE'S SAAAAAFE! OH MY GOLLY WILCOX GOT THREE BASES ON A BUNT! NEVER BEFORE IN THE HISTORY OF THE GAME HAVE I SEEN THIS! HAPPY ON THIRD, WILCOX TIPS HIS CAP TO THE SCREAMING CROWD!"

Plan #4
Better plan...

Plan # 5
Way worse plan...

Plan #6

Hmmmmmm...

"Zip Tuggle here! The great Willie Mays steps up to the plate! Wilcox on third. And — OH MY GOLLY, WILCOX IS <u>STEALING HOME</u>! EVERY GIANTS FAN IS ON HIS FEET! Mays can't believe it! Here's the throw at the plate as Wilcox SLIDES in a cloud of dust. He's safe! No, he's out! No, HE'S SAFE! SAFE AT HOME AFTER THREE BASES ON A BUNT AND WILLIE MAYS IS HUGGING WILCOX AND THE CROWD IS GOING WILD! WILCOX HAS <u>WON</u> <u>THE PENNANT</u> FOR THE SAN FRANCISCO GIANTS! OH MY GOLLY GEE!"

Oh!
That might work.

What if ~~[scribbled out text]~~
~~[scribbled out text]~~
~~[scribbled out text]~~
~~[scribbled out text]~~

I wouldn't put it past her to sneak
into my bedroom and find this diary.
Yipes!

What do you think Carleton'd think bout
my plan? Or Drusie? Should I tell her?
What if she rats me out to Mrs. Ravenbach?

Can you trust a girl?

Once upon a time, Mrs. Ravenbach was a
girl.

No she wasn't.
She was always a prison camp guard.
Even when she was five.

Think I'll tell Drusie.
Who Dares, Wins!

thanks for listening,
your pal,
Toby

CHAPTER 14

When you are a tall and wonderfully sculpted person such as myself, finding an easy place to hide for the eavesdropping is not a simple matter. My firm bosom and wonderfully large, round, hard belly make it a little bit difficult to conceal all of me, ha-ha.

As you may know, my favorite spot to do the eavesdropping is the coatrack in the hallway outside my classroom. There is always a row of rain boots scattered messily on the floor under the coats, then there are the coats on the hooks, and a shelf for hats and book bags and notebooks and backpacks and things that are important to fourth grade children. I have learned that if I stand with my feet behind the rain boots, and hide behind the coats, my round belly is not noticeable. At least, no child has yet remarked upon it when I was hiding behind the coats in my favorite eavesdropping spot. Students sometimes are so naive!

So it was one bright and sunny Monday afternoon at the semester's end, a few days before the All-School Poetry Contest at the McKegway School for Clever and Gifted Children, that I found myself in my favorite eavesdropping spot patiently waiting to see what random conversation might be had between any two of my students.

It is incredible sometimes what a teacher can observe when the students are unaware that the teacher is watching. Students should realize that the teacher is always, always watching!

I heard loud, thundering footsteps in the hallway. Bald-headed Richard came down the hall picking his nose. I can assure you, I have never needed to pick my nose in my entire life. And were I to pick my nose, I would take care to use a lace handkerchief. One has no idea what kind of pestilence might be introduced into the temple that is one's body if one were to put a bare finger up one's nose. What an unpleasant thought!

Most of Richard's finger had disappeared inside his head as if he were searching for a misplaced chunk of gold.

I heard Richard say, "Hey, Toby!"

"Yo, Richard. We gonna have a Sub Club meeting Saturday?"

"We should, but I don't think Arthur's ready with his drawings."

Despite hours and hours and *hours* of Tobias's and Richard's and Arthur's lunch table discussion of submarine design, I was quite certain that no submarine would *ever* be built by *these* three. Maybe a leaky dinghy for Stuart Little built of the popsicle sticks, but not a fully functional U-boat, and certainly not a craft worthy of the name *Kriegsmarine*!!!

Sometimes boys are the dumbest things in the world!

It was then, peering between two rather smelly coats, that I noticed Richard had an iPod.

Tobias said, "Cool!"

"What?"

"When'd you get an iPod? I thought your parents said you couldn't have one, and wouldn't give you the money."

"Um. Ah."

I felt my blood freeze. It was all I could do to keep from bursting from my hiding place and yanking Richard out of that hallway like a movie stuntman jerked by a wire after he's been shot. One problem with a super-secret eavesdropping spot is that you cannot break from the sanctuary of your eavesdropping spot or the student will know you are doing the eavesdropping! This would not be popular with the parents or the principal of your school.

Richard mumbled, "Um. Err."

"Where'd you get it? Your grandmother die or something?"

"No, man. She made us brownies last week."

"Where on earth did you get an iPod? They're real expensive!"

Richard's little lower lip was trembling. He was so pathetic, I wanted to slap him hard across his face. It is sad that, in the United States, they do not allow teachers to slap the children on their face. Education would move forward with much more speed but the teacher's hand would often get covered with jelly, or dirt, or sticky marshmallow goo.

It was at that point that Richard Kaliski began to shake.

"What?"

"Nothing."

"You kidding? Nothing? Something's up! What's the problem, man? Tell me what it is. That's what friends're for."

Richard began to shake harder. I knew this was not going to

go well for me, but there was not a thing I could do but stand there, hidden behind the coats like a *Dummkopf.*

Tobias reached his fat little arms forward and hugged his friend. Seeing little boys hugging one another made my skin crawl. Boys are not supposed to be hugging other boys. Boys are supposed to be throwing javelins at one another. Boys did not hug other boys during the Third Reich!

Tobias said, "What's the matter?"

"M—M— Mrs. Ravenbach . . . she . . ." he could not go on, the sap.

"She what?"

Richard took a great, big, giant, deep breath. He had taken such a deep breath, I felt I could see his toes swelling up. "I'm so, so sorry. I'm sorry. I did a terrible thing. I'm so sorry! Please tell me you'll forgive me!"

Dismayed, Tobias stepped back from his friend. I was so pleased.

"What've you done? What has Mrs. Ravenbach done?!"

"She, she, she pays me to tell her what you're doing."

"That's the stupidest thing I ever heard of."

Richard was wailing like a *Luftalarm* air raid siren. "THAT'S HOW I GOT THE MONEY TO BUY THE IPOD!"

"What'd you tell her?!"

"Stuff."

Stuff? If they ever wanted to take over the world, children needed lessons in the use of specific information. Fortunately they do not desire very much the world domination, or they would have better organization and far better grammar.

Richard said, "I told her your parents were mad at you, and

also about your crush on Drusie, and a bunch of other dumb stuff, and . . . and . . . I gave her your journal." He howled in agony.

Tobias stood back, his jaw hanging down in complete surprise. Naturally, he looked like a moron because he had at that instant discovered he had been betrayed by his best friend.

"You ratted me out to Mrs. Ravenbach! For money?! That's the worst thing I ever heard!"

"She told me if I didn't do what she said, she'd make me repeat fourth grade. I feel so horrible."

"You should."

He drew back his arm. Tobias was about to hit him. It was a moment of delicious anticipation for me, the teacher.

Then young Tobias Wilcox did something I did not think he had the gumption to do. He hugged his friend again, even harder. He hugged the person who had betrayed him. The idiot.

Tobias said, "She's awful. I'd've done the same thing. You're lucky she didn't sit on you." Bald-headed Richard, his finger wet from having just been up his nose, wiped his eyes with that same wet finger, and stood in the hallway hugging his friend. I was embarrassed for him. Tobias said, "It's okay. She's sooooo awful."

"Yeah. With retch-o bad breath."

"And smelly feet."

"And a big bumpy brown mole with hair growing out of it on her *face*." Tobias laughed. He laughed about the mole of which I am so proud! Richard laughed too. Richard said, "Big bumpy brown mole!"

Tobias said, "Big bumpy brown mole!" and they bumped their hips together like dancing.

"*Big* bumpy brown mole!"

"Big bumpy *brown* mole!"

"Big *bumpy* brown mole!"

"BIG BUMPY BROWN MOLE!"

"*BIG* BUMPY BROWN MOLE!"

"WITH HAIR GROWING OUT OF IT!!!"

"WITH HAIR GROWING OUT OF IT!!!!"

"ON HER *FACE*!!!"

"ON HER *FACE*!!!"

They laughed like the fools that they were. I desperately wanted to step out from my hiding place, bash their heads together, and strangle them with their belts. I refrained.

It was most unpleasant. First the nose picking. Then the hugging. Then the forgiveness, which came as an awful surprise. Then the business about my wonderful mole. Then the laughing. Especially the laughing.

All of it terribly dispiriting for me, a teacher.

Several times during the next days, to my great displeasure, I saw bald-headed little Richard whispering with young Tobias Wilcox. Several times when they were whispering, I had the unpleasant sensation, like the spiders crawling up my back, that they were whispering about me. Being whispered about is a vaguely unsettling feeling that is not altogether *wunderbar*. There is nothing about the whispering that *is* pleasant. Unless, of course, one is doing the whispering oneself.

CHAPTER 15

At last the morning came that we had all been waiting for. The annual McKegway School for Clever and Gifted Children All-School Poetry Contest!

Once a year, in the gymnasium, a new King or Queen of Poetry is crowned. The child who is crowned Queen or King of Poetry is praised to the heavens and showered with a lifetime of glory and honor. It is the Academy Award, the Nobel Prize, and the MacArthur Genius Grant all rolled into one. When your most humble narrator was a child in East Germany, she won the *Grundschule* Poetry Contest and was heaped with honor and glory. There is nothing like a wonderful boost for a child's ego, early in life, to send her on the wonderful path of the teaching and the scholarly appreciation. That warm feeling of triumph is a memory I treasure to this day.

The morning was boiling hot, but all the children were dressed in their finest clothes. Little patent leather Mary Janes shined. Hair tied neatly in beautiful pink bows. Lace-up shoes polished. Jackets and ties. No food on any shirts! It was a glorious, glorious morning. All the school was there. The parents. The teachers. Not the staff, of course. The grandparents. Even the children of the custodians were in their nicest frocks and overalls. The mood was festive. *Fröhlich.* Upbeat.

It was as wonderful a day as is possible to imagine.

Well, not totally.

When you work at a place with only one German employee, things can quite easily get into disarray. The McKegway School for Clever and Gifted Children was no exception to this ironclad rule. Children were running every which way. Teachers were yelling. Parents were wondering where they should sit. Grandparents were staggering around and bashing people with their canes. There was actually even a dog in the back of the gymnasium, barking. Not one solitary person had the presence of mind to take it outside and lock it in a hot automobile.

The gymnasium, on a blistering day in June, was a festival of disgusting smells, most of them involving the sweat. I was certain that, behind a bleacher somewhere, a sweaty child was throwing up.

From my seat where I was doing my knitting surrounded by my beloved pupils, my sharp and clever eyes noticed a man looking at me from across the room. I was not sure who this man was, but I felt that, once upon a time, he may have been a student of mine. So many attractive men had been my students at one time or the other.

The beastly dog's incessant barking was getting on my nerves. The yelling of the children, the moaning of their parents, the hysterical screeching of the grandparents wandering lost, were getting on my nerves. What I needed was a bottle of *Schnaps* and a fistful of tranquilizers.

Mr. Hertenstein took his position on the stage. Everyone instantly got quiet like dead bunny rabbits. It would be wonderful to be the principal of a school and be able to make seven hundred people become quiet and still simply by stepping up to a podium!

Even more wonderful than winning a Golden Apple the fifth time for Excellence in Teaching at the McKegway School for Clever and Gifted Children, I must confess, it would be deliciously wonderful to become the *principal* of the McKegway School for Clever and Gifted Children. This was a thought I almost never allowed myself to think. Sometimes when he had a few brandies, Mr. Ravenbach would have this thought and speak it out loud to me. I would always say, "Tut-tut" and say no more about it.

But, deep inside, I must confess, a tiny flame did burn.

Perhaps, if Tobias Wilcox *won* the All-School Poetry Contest...

Handsome Mr. Hertenstein said, "It's fantastic to be gathered here today for the annual McKegway All-School Poetry Contest. Each and every child wrote and learned his or her own poem all by themselves, from kindergartener to eighth-grader. Isn't that fabulous?!" Mr. Hertenstein applauded vigorously. Everyone applauded vigorously. Everyone wanted the principal to adore them.

My applause was the loudest.

"Will the children who won for their grade please come onstage to say your poem for the All-School Poetry Contest. Kindergarten on my right, eighth grade on my left." More joyful applause.

Mine was the most joyful. I am certain Mr. Hertenstein was pleased.

The nine children stood up and awkwardly threaded their way down front, then up the steps to the stage and a row of hard wooden chairs.

Susie Clementine sat first. So adorable with her pink shoes. Followed by first grader Matteen Taheri. Then, for the second grade, Alejandro Gonzales. Third grade was rather poorly represented by Amanda Pennington. Then, as you are quite well aware, along came young Tobias Wilcox, representing the fourth grade, and in particular, the wonderful classroom of wonderful Mrs. Leni Ravenbach. *Wunderbar!*

As he marched up on that glorious stage, young Tobias Wilcox was *radiant.* Positively, extravagantly, radiant! I had never seen a more handsome boy. And, in this flattering light, such an interesting thing, can you believe it? He did not look even the *slightest* bit fat!

I felt quite an outpouring of love and affection and tenderness and caring for my young pupil. His poem was, like his adoring teacher, *wunderbar!*

Other than the ceaseless barking of the insane dog, it was a glorious, glorious day! Making altogether too much noise, the fifth, sixth, seventh, and eighth grade students took their place onstage to the right of young Tobias Wilcox. The longer they had been away from the orderly classroom of Mrs. Leni Ravenbach, the more scruffy, less pleasant, and less presentable each child had become! Truly, the eighth-grader looked as if he had been dragged out of a polluted river after a month underwater.

No one could be quiet. I was so deeply embarrassed for Principal Hertenstein. How marvelous he looked in his three-piece dark gray suit and bright cardinal-and-gold tie, standing before the parents, the grandparents, and that horrid barking dog! He raised his hand, gently, quietly, and with scarcely a noticeable motion. Everyone in the sweltering gymnasium was instantly silent. Including the dog.

"Shall we begin?"

As Larry Dooling, the *McKegway Gazette* reporter, made notes on his little notepad, the first little girl, the one in the kindergarten, did a fine job. She did not pee-pee in her ruffly underwear or vomit. Quite the improvement over the kindergarten poetry learners in years past!

I rubbed my big, hard belly and waited with great anticipation for the first-grader and the second-grader and the third-grader to start and finish their poems. I was so pleased that I had been able to reach young Tobias Wilcox and been able to help him, and that he had seen the light of day and realized a warm, wonderful poem about his beloved *Grossvater* would be the best thing in the world for him, his parents, and his future.

The first grade child and second grade child, they did well. Actually, not so well. The first grade child could not stop looking at himself on the big video screens, and the second grade child forgot the words to his poem and had to be reminded six times. Finally, he cried and sat down. How awful for Mrs. Jiang, his teacher! I observed her bright red face and her shame. She should have drilled him more. Then she would not have been embarrassed in front of everybody in the whole, entire world.

The third grade child, the less said about her and her idiotic poem, the better.

At last came the grand moment for which we all had been waiting.

Mr. Hertenstein said, "Representing Mrs. Ravenbach's fourth grade classroom, Toby Wilcox." The amount of applause young Tobias received while stumbling to the center of the stage was disconcerting. I had no idea the child was so popular.

He removed his baseball hat and put his hands behind his back like Abraham Lincoln. He looked around the room. He looked at me. His teacher.

Inside, I felt warm and peaceful. A sweet poem about a beloved grandfather . . . *wunderbar*!

What then came out of his mouth was not what I was expecting. I will never forget a word of it. Not in a million years.

He said, "This is called 'My Teacher.' I wrote all of it myself." He was smiling an enormous amount. His teeth looked like piano keys. He was smiling more, in fact, than I'd ever seen a child smile in my entire teaching career.

He began to recite his awful poem.

"Her crowning glory is her golden hair;
We wish her manners were equally fair.
She lectures that the worst thing is a liar,
But our classroom smells of her pants on fire.
She goes on and on about what we lack,
While she 'invented' Mr. Ravenbach.
I bet she made him up, who knows why . . ."

Everyone was sitting up straight. No one was breathing. Each and every person in that hot, stinky gymnasium was drinking in the awful *Dreck* Tobias Wilcox was reciting as if it were the nectar of the gods.

I regarded their faces.

They were believing what the odious child was saying.

The room began to swim and swirl. I tried to raise my wonderful self from the rickety chair. My until-now-reliable muscles were not helping. A taste of panic spread through me like slow fire, not unlike five shots of *Schnaps*.

Then, from across the dark gymnasium, I saw a tiny woman slicing ahead like hot acid through a sea of dirty little ants. Mrs. Button! My dear friend! Coming forward with an expression of righteous anger that made my heart swell in my great, firm bosom. I could see that she had something she wanted to share with one and all. The look of venomous hatred on her face said it was going to be directed at young Tobias Wilcox, her across-the-street neighbor and tubby nemesis. She was going to give him *a piece of her mind*!

The moment, the day, the entire school year would be handed back to me, as I so richly deserved. Victory was about to be mine.

Disgusting, fat, repugnant, reprehensible, and not too bright Tobias Wilcox took a deep breath and bellowed, "Mrs. Button! You stop right there! Don't you even open your tiny little mouth with your dead-person lipstick! It doesn't matter how rich you are, nobody in this entire gym wants to hear what you have to say! Your kids graduated forever ago and you're not even a parent here! You only came to get me in trouble and tell lies to help your fat friend Mrs. Ravenbach! Don't come over to my house! You only pretend to be my mom's buddy! Don't ask her if you can borrow sugar, or butter, or a loaf of bread, or two eggs! I don't ever want any more of your stupid brownies!"

"Why . . . you impertinent . . . little twerp," Mrs. Button stammered.

"Get outta here! This's not your school! It's *mine*!"

The entire student body, they clapped! Apparently, the bitter feeling young Tobias Wilcox held for his across-the-street neighbor was shared by all of the children. This came as quite the surprise, as she was a totally delightful woman. Who made such lovely tea cakes.

My dear friend, Mrs. Button, was, for the first time since I'd known her, unable to say a single, solitary word. Not one! With all the blood boiling inside her, her eyes were about to explode.

As she walked away, her lovely dress seemed to grow three sizes as she shrank just a little. Pushing on the gymnasium door, she pivoted and stared at everyone with hateful black rage. The expression on her sharp-toothed face was the most poisonous, the most vengeful I had seen on any face, ever.

Even my own when I practiced in the mirror.

As the gymnasium door clapped shut behind my dear, dear friend, I resolved, the next time we had tea, to give her an extra lump of sugar. She deserved it.

Like the *Tirpitz*'s twin 38-centimeter deck guns revolving to face a tender target, my attention to young Tobias Wilcox I directed.

Knitting clutched to my marvelous bosom, my fashionable

French high-heeled shoes made a wonderful thundering sound as toward the stage I marched. Tobias Wilcox's poetry-reciting voice was extraordinarily clear and painfully loud, and, worse, could be heard by every person and dog in the gymnasium, as he said . . .

> "She's so compelled to lie, lie, lie
> About me stealing her dumb brush and comb;
> THE PENITENTIARY SHOULD BE HER HOME.
> WHEN PEOPLE ASK ME WHAT I LEARNED
>   IN SCHOOL—"
> I'LL TELL THEM SHE TAUGHT US HOW TO
>   BE CRUEL.
> BUT I COULD PROBABLY FORGIVE HER LIES
> IF, MR. HERTENSTEIN, SHE'LL APOLOGIZE."

My face hurt, my ankles hurt. My chest hurt. I was afraid I was going to fall down like a giant redwood tree, dead of a heart attack. Encouragingly toward our principal I looked, but he remained maddeningly silent. I yelled at Tobias, "SIT DOWN. NOW."

He said, in a most irritating tone, "I will not."

"Mr. Hertenstein, YOU MUST STOP THAT BOY!"

Principal Hertenstein said, "Why?"

Tobias scrunched his little fat-cheeked face and said impertinently, "Why should he stop me?"

If there is one solitary thing that makes me lose *all* sense of the order and the discipline, it is being sneered at by an inferior.

"YOU HAVE VIOLATED THE FIRST RULE OF THE ALL-SCHOOL POETRY CONTEST!" I was breathing so hard.

His little voice was soooo syrupy nasty. "What rule was *that*, Mrs. Ravenbach?"

"EVERY CHILD'S POEM IS REQUIRED TO COME FROM THE WRITING THAT EACH STUDENT CRE-ATED IN HIS OR HER JOURNAL!" From my mouth, spittle flicked.

He sounded too sweet, like Rebecca of Sunnybrook Farm. Too sweet. "I wrote in my journal just like everybody else."

Unable to keep the victory from my voice, I deeply inhaled. My wonderful chest expanded. "YOU KNOW AS WELL AS I DO THAT ALL THE ENTIRE SEMESTER LONG, NOT *ONE SINGLE WORD* OF THIS HORRID POEM WAS *EVER* MENTIONED IN YOUR PRIVATE JOURN—"

The entire gymnasium went as silent as the Lakehurst Naval Air Station the morning after the *Hindenburg* disaster . . .

I had made a terrible mistake.

My first.

Fat little Tobias Wilcox's deep, scratchy voice floated out above the heads of every person in the gymnasium. "Mrs. Raven-bach, you . . . read . . . my . . . *journal*." His voice was as lethal and precise as a hypodermic needle filled with the potassium cyanide. He almost sounded German.

At me every child was looking. No one cares what the students think.

At me every parent was looking. No one cares what the parents think unless it's time to get the tuition check.

Our beloved principal, Mr. Hertenstein, was looking at

me most intently. He was the one I most didn't want looking at me.

Into a walkie-talkie Richard spoke. "Now hear this. This is the Commander of the *Red October.*" The strange man across the room picked up his own walkie-talkie and listened as Richard said, "Proceed toward target at flank speed." The vaguely familiar man set down his walkie-talkie and moved toward me.

I said, "Tobias Wilcox, there is no way I could have known what was in your confidential private journal! Teachers do not read their students' personal, confidential, private journals!"

"You did."

The strange man reached me.

I said, "And how such a thing could you *possibly* be thinking?!"

Tobias Wilcox said, "I've known it a long time, but who'd believe a kid, so we gave it to Mr. Grossinger, and guess what?! He found your nasty teacher *fingerprints* all over my personal, confidential, private journal! WHO DARES, WINS!"

"We . . . who is this 'we'?"

The man squeezed my arm. A bit harshly. I inspected him. He was wearing, I must admit, a lovely dark blue worsted wool suit.

"And who might you be?!"

"Eddie LeJeune."

Every child shouted, "FAST EDDIE?!"

"Mrs. Ravenbach, I am no longer Fast Eddie LeJeune . . . I am the Honorable Edward T. LeJeune. I am a federal judge."

Every child in the gymnasium *screamed.*

The dog barked so much, it threw up on a kindergartener.

Tobias put on his nasty hat, jumped off the stage, and directly toward me he ran.

I had a terrible creeping sensation that the order and the discipline were going to become something that only existed in the past and the past was coming very quickly.

Mr. Hertenstein said, "Mrs. Ravenbach? What do you have to say for yourself?"

"I am an educator! Why would I lie?!"

Right in front of me, Tobias did a ridiculous little happy dance and said, "Because you are a yucky human being! You put those hairbrushes and comb and mirror in my desk and pretended someone saw me, just to get me in trouble! Didn't you?!" When I said nothing, he shrieked, "DIDN'T YOU?!!" *Natürlich,* I kept mum. There was always a chance he would be struck by the lightning.

Tobias said, "Mr. Hertenstein, I got something I gotta tell everybody at the McKegway School! Federal Judge Edward T. LeJeune did *not* repeat fourth grade and has *never been in a penitentiary!*"

From the audience, came the cheers. Cheers! I could not believe it.

The next time you mention someone being in the penitentiary, make sure that person is well and truly cold in their grave. It makes for fewer unpleasant confrontations, such as that one.

Pupils and former pupils from all directions squeezed in— like a vice. Fourth-graders, fifth-graders, sixth-graders, seventh-graders, eighth-graders, and also parents, grandparents, and custodians! There were even parents who many years ago in my class had been students. It felt like the witch trials in Salem. Or Joan of Arc, right at the end.

"Who'd ever want to kiss you?!"

"With your stinky mole!"

"How come you never got fired?!"

"You're mean and you're ugly and you smell like farts!"

"You ruined my son's *life!*"

"I hated brushing your hair, it was the most disgusting thing I've ever done!"

"No, no! The most disgusting thing was rubbing her icky feet!"

Tobias Wilcox said, "I never touched her nasty old gross feet!"

Federal Judge Edward T. LeJeune said, "Neither did I, Toby. You and I share a lot in common. We should have lunch sometime."

The sea of bright red, angry faces gave me the awful sensation that they were chanting, "Burn her! Burn her! Burn her!"

I decided it was best to be elsewhere.

As I staggered toward the McKegway School for Clever and Gifted Children gymnasium doors, I saw fat, disgusting, deceitful, wretched, and most decidedly unpleasant Tobias Wilcox being kissed by Drusilla Tanner on his dirty cheek and being lifted on the shoulders of his classmates like a Roman emperor or a World Cup goalkeeper, amid hurrahs, huzzahs, hoorays, and overall tumults of exultation.

"Toby! Toby! Toby! Toby Toby Toby Toby TOBY!!"

Never have I ever seen a child so happy. His chums, at their teacher, began to laugh.

I left.

Even as the heavy metal doors slammed behind me, I could hear them laughing.

As I squeezed into my Volkswagen, I could hear them laughing.

And I can hear them laughing still.

"WHO DARES WINS!" I highly recommend it.

CHAPTER 16

The last day of that endless school year, it was gray and awful and poured rain.

Not one child cared.

As they sprinted up the hallway to the front doors for the last carpool, the children squealed about how they were going to burn their schoolbooks, or shoot them with the shotguns, or throw them at homeless people from their mothers' automobiles. All the parents were excited too.

Usually, I was loving the last day because the students would always come up to me and smile, and give me precious little gifts, and tell me how much they loved being in my homeroom.

This year, that did not happen.

Not one single student came up to me in the carpool line to say, "Thank you, Mrs. Ravenbach. You are the finest teacher I've ever had in my entire life. I am so lucky to have had you as a teacher, because now I know my life will turn out to be fine."

Not this year. Sadly.

I saw young Tobias Wilcox dump his wonderful schoolbooks into the trash receptacle by the driveway. He was smiling.

Lately, he had been smiling quite often. Probably because, after the commotion had subsided at the All-School Poetry Contest and the fifth-grader, sixth-grader, seventh-grader, and eighth-grader said their poems, the judges awarded the King of Poetry prize to young Tobias Wilcox. It turned out that he *had* written his ghastly "My Teacher" poem in his journal—in teensy tiny handwriting that only a fourth-grader could possibly see. I only wish that, instead of crowning him King of Poetry, they had stoned him to death.

Especially since Mr. Hertenstein mounted a vigorous campaign to get me sacked.

Tobias ran toward the carpool line.

His father lifted one of those boom box things onto the roof of his automobile. He pressed "play" and that *horrible* song BLASTED across campus. Sung by that horrible long-haired man with all the runny eyeliner.

"School's out . . . for summer!
School's out . . . forever!"

All the children and all the parents and all the teachers sang along with the horrible song. When they sang about the McKegway School for Clever and Gifted Children being exploded all the teachers were laughing.

Tobias veered toward me, smiling a smile from his left ear to his right ear. I knew, deep in my heart, that he was coming to apologize for his wretched behavior. A warm feeling flowed through me for the little child.

I knelt down, spread my arms to embrace him. He stopped ten feet away and jammed his right hand in a little fist, shoving it toward me. And then, he flipped up his middle finger and *shot me the bird*!

I looked around. No one had noticed. Young Tobias Wilcox gave his wonderful, wonderful teacher the finger and *no one saw*. He was not going to get in trouble.

It broke my heart.

All this limp American parenting and lax behavior and pathetic lack of the order and the discipline! Because of the deficiencies in his upbringing, I am certain that young Tobias Wilcox will end his days looking through stainless-steel bars in a maximum-security penitentiary, probably in Nevada.

That grim future was far from his mind.

As he whirled around and bounced to his father's open arms, he was thinking only about summertime.

Dear Willie,

School's been out a while. Yay!
Sorry haven't written lately. Too many things
to do. and see. Happy to fill you in on
the high points.

Nice to say what's on my mind. I won't
ever stop. I bet you say what's on your
mind. You seem like that kind of a guy.

Turns out, Mr. Hertenstein told old Mrs.
Ravenbach her nasty behavior meant
she wasn't eligible for the Teacher of the
Year award. Ha! I bet when she heard
that, black smoke came shooting out her
ears. Ha ha! As my Papi would say,
"Sure fixed her little red wagon!"

Went camping for a week with my dad.
He taught me how to cook rib eye steak.
We ate steak every night. Mom wasn't
there to stop us. Tee hee.

My parents took me and Richard to
Disneyland. Rode Space Mountain four
times. Threw up behind Redd Rockett's
Pizza Port. Twice.

Me and Drusie went to a James Bond
film festival. Saw Thunderball. The best
one. We shared a box of Milk Duds. She
let me hold her hand in the dark. Her
hand pulled back after a little while,
but still, it felt real nice. What'd it be
like to hold her hand as long as I
wanted? Wouldn't that be the greatest?

Saw Mrs. Button at the grocery Store. Went up to her, stuck my finger in my nose and dug out a big booger. Flipped it at her. When she wasn't looking.

The Sub Club (me and Richard, Arthur, Trevania, _and_ Drusie!) finished our submarine, the "Nautilus" and had a regatta at Lake Ruppenthal. Really awesome test. The Alka-Seltzer dissolved perfectly, releasing the ballast and "Nautilus" surfaced according to plan. Good to have a plan.

Carleton came to visit for the regatta. He and Richard and Drusie all got along great. It was awesome to see him. He said I was more relaxed than I'd sounded in my emails.

This summer, I get to play Big League Sandlot baseball! Kid pitch! I hope I get number 24. How cool would that be?

Next year, I'll be in fifth grade. Hopefully I won't have to play on Mckegway's rotten football team. Worst team, ever.

I sure won't ever have to have lunch with Mrs. Ravenbach again. Ever, ever.

I'd like to have lunch with you sometime.

thanks for listening
your pal,

Toby

CHAPTER 17

It would be nice, I think, if there were a real Mr. Ravenbach. It is difficult to live alone. Sometimes it is wonderful that no one tells me what to do, or how to think. Sometimes it is sad.

My consolation is that I have my students.

And, *natürlich*, my dear friend Mrs. Button.

It is so, so helpful for a teacher to have a thoughtful *Freundin* on the board of directors of the school where one is teaching! And so, like a gangster quietly disappearing into the witness protection program, any silly talk of Mrs. Ravenbach and her beloved job parting ways . . . gently . . . *vanished. Wunderbar!*

I will have a wonderful summer planning my course curriculum, content in the knowledge that, come September, I will have a homeroom filled with new, eager, delightful, wonderful students. Next year's children will be my best pupils ever. All happy, well dressed, and eager to learn what Mrs. Ravenbach wishes to teach them . . . everything they need to become the wonderful adult citizens, far, far from the penitentiary.

Next year will be the year I shall win my fifth Golden Apple Award for Excellence in Teaching at the McKegway School for Clever and Gifted Children!

I do so love being a teacher.

THE END

Toby Wilcox will return to do battle with Stormin' Norman — Greatest Baseball Coach in the World!

HELPFUL GLOSSARY

Apfelstrudel: apple strudel ... like apple pie, but sooooooooo *much* better

Bratwurst: tasty, spicy, beautifully prepared link sausage, often handmade

Dirndl: German woman's traditional dress, very flattering

Dummkopf: idiot, moron, clod, imbecile, dim-bulb loser, dunce, nincompoop, ignoramus, dummy, *schmuck*, and my favorite ... retard

Dreck: icky mess

Eins, zwei, drei: one, two, three

Freund: friend, of whom I have many

Fröhlich: happy, which I am ... nearly all of the time

Fritten: fried potatoes, but certainly not French!

Gott im Himmel: God in heaven

Grossmutter: Grandmother

Grossvater: Grandfather

Grundschule: grade school . . . a wonderful place to spend the time

Ja: yes!

Kartoffelsalat: potato salad, extremely delicious!

Kindergarten: take a wild guess

Kiste: butt (a word I find coarse and unpleasant)

Mach schnell: hurry up!

Müsli: a delightful breakfast dish made with oatmeal, grain, dried fruit, seeds, nuts, and milk . . . *so* wonderful!

Natürlich: naturally

Nichts: nothing (what's in some boys' heads)

Opa: Granddaddy

Schnaps: very strong alcoholic beverage, flavored with fruit! Yum!

Schauer: shiver

Spätlese Riesling: a particularly lovely type of German white wine

Waffen-SS: Nazi party soldiers in WWII

Wehrmacht: all German armed forces in WWII

Wunderbar: wonderful, my *favorite* word

Würstchen: small sausage, quite yummy!

THANK YOU!

Kelly Catron, who (when everyone told me I shouldn't write a book told from the bad guy's point of view) read an early draft, *got* it, and encouraged me like a house afire. I'd never have fought on without your crucial boost.

Craig Phillips for the beach house, Hilary Bell, Donna Koppelman, Pam Casey, Tracy Barrett, Suzanne Kingsbury, Chris Ruppenthal, Cheryl Klein, Richard Beban, Ruta Sepetys, Marti Young, Kurt Hampe, Josh Bledsoe, Wesley Cook, Will Robinson, Alexandra Bowen, my stellar editor Alexis Gargagliano, and FIP (finest radio station, ever).

Bruce Cohen, who suggested I send the manuscript to his buddy Judith Regan.

And Judith, who loved it.

AUTHOR BIO

William M. Akers thinks writing books is a ton more fun than actual work. This is his first novel. Buy your friends a bunch of copies so he can write more.

tobywilcox.com